HOT ANGEL

Hostile Operations Team - Book 12

LYNN RAYE HARRIS

The Hostile Operations Team® and Lynn Raye Harris® are trademarks of H.O.T. Publishing, LLC.

Printed in the United States of America

First Printing, 2018

For rights inquires, visit www.LynnRayeHarris.com

HOT Angel
Copyright © 2018 by Lynn Raye Harris
Cover Design Copyright © 2018 Croco Designs

ISBN: 978-1-941002-27-8

Chapter 1

"You okay, honey?"

Brooke Sullivan turned her head at the sound of her best friend's voice. Grace Campbell Spencer sat in the chair beside her, frowning. Brooke pasted on a smile that she hoped didn't shake at the corners.

"Of course I am. Why?"

Grace didn't look convinced. "You seemed far away for a second."

Brooke twirled the stem of her margarita glass. "I'm fine. Just thinking."

Grace's frown didn't ease. From the next room, shouts erupted. Brooke flinched so hard she jarred the glass and spilled some of her drink. Grace didn't miss anything, of course. She stood and marched toward the great room where the men were watching football, her expression stern.

"Grace, no," Brooke called after her. "It's okay. They just startled me."

"I'm going to tell them to keep it down."

Brooke bounded up and caught her friend by the elbow. Grace was a lot taller, a lot more elegant. But she stopped and stared down at Brooke with concern.

"Please don't." Brooke swallowed. Hard. "I have to get used to it. It's been almost two years."

She hated saying how long it had been since she'd been abducted by the terrorist group because it made her sound so pitiful. Two years and she still wasn't over it? Two years and she couldn't act normal when a group of men roared at a football game on television? How pathetic was that?

About as pathetic as the fact she'd given up her house, moved into a condo building because it had a secure entrance, and gotten a dog. Oh, and then there was the fact she'd quit her dream job—well, sold her dream business, actually—and started a consulting business from home. Because then she wouldn't have to leave the house every day if she didn't want to.

Grace folded her arms and frowned. But then she nodded and they returned to their seats at the island in Grace's expansive kitchen. The other women were in the next room with the men, watching the game and eating snacks, but Grace had settled the two of them in here. Probably because she knew that a room filled with as much testosterone as a group of commandos put off was way too much for Brooke.

Grace picked up her vodka and tonic and took a sip. "Can you keep a secret?"

"Are you kidding me? I'm your best friend. Why would you ask me that?" Brooke was almost offended.

Grace set her drink down. "That's not vodka. Or tonic. It's Sprite."

"Why would you drink Sprite and pretend it's vodka — Oh." Brooke put a hand to her mouth. "You're pregnant," she whispered. "Oh my God, you're pregnant!"

Grace nodded as tears filled her eyes. "Garrett and I didn't want to tell anyone yet. We need to tell Cammie first. But he won't mind if I tell you. Just keep it quiet, okay?"

Brooke hugged her friend tight. "Of course I won't tell anyone. Will Cammie be excited?"

Cammie was Garrett's daughter from a previous marriage. Her mother was a stone-cold bitch, but Cammie was a good kid. She visited often and spent a couple of months every summer. But Brooke didn't really know her all that well or how she might take the news.

"Garrett says so. I think so. But we want to ease her into it. Tell her it won't affect her relationship with her dad or how much he loves her. It'll be hard since she's still in Georgia with her mother most of the time, but Melissa seems to have toned down the vitriol now that she's in a new relationship."

Brooke scoffed. "Really? You two geniuses think it's her relationship with a new man that's making Garrett's ex be reasonable? You're the daughter of the president of the United States. Garrett is his son-in-law. She makes nice because of the status it probably gives her in her hometown."

Grace pursed her lips. "Probably. I keep expecting to see her splashed all over the front pages of a tabloid, quite honestly, telling her story. Whatever that may be."

"Yeah, well, nobody believes those things anyway."

There was another shout from the great room. Brooke managed not to spill her drink this time. "See, getting better all the time."

Grace squeezed her arm. "I know, sweetie." She slipped from the chair. "And now that I've told you the news, you won't be surprised when I tell you I have to pee."

"Nope." Not that Brooke had personal experience, but she had a sister. And she'd had coworkers and other friends who'd been pregnant.

"Don't go anywhere," Grace commanded.

"I won't. Promise."

Grace hurried down the hall to the half bath. Brooke closed her eyes and let out a sigh. She hated this helplessness. This rage and fear. She'd gone to counseling, dammit. She'd worked hard to fix her life, and she didn't let the fear stop her. Well, most of the time anyway.

So what if she'd made changes? Maybe they were needed changes. She *liked* working from home. And she got out socially because Grace made her. So it wasn't all that bad, right?

She heard footsteps and spun around. A tall, dark-haired man with muscles that went on for days stood with a beer in his hand and gazed back at her.

Cade.

"Hi," she said, her heart pounding.

"Hi. How've you been?"

4

Brooke laughed nervously. But was it because he was big and tough and capable of violence? Or because he made butterflies swirl in her belly?

"Fine. Nothing's changed since the last time I saw you."

"Which was a week ago at Buddy's."

"Yes." She'd seen this man half a dozen times over the past month, each time for a few minutes only, but she still remembered the first time. At Colonel Mendez's wedding last month when she'd been drunk and angry with herself for being so pitiful. She hadn't had sex in forever, hadn't felt a man's touch or the comfort of being held close, and her inhibitions were down because she'd had too much champagne. If Garrett and Grace hadn't shown up when they did, she probably would have gone home with Cade Rodgers.

And she didn't know how that would have turned out because she still had so many issues she might have freaked out in the middle of the whole thing. Or maybe she'd have been thrilled she'd gotten over her fear of big men who lived lives of violence—but probably she'd have run home and locked herself away for days.

He ambled closer, heading around the island and depositing the beer bottle on the counter. He took another from the fridge and popped the top. But he didn't hurry back to the other room.

"You don't say much, do you, Brooke?"

"I…" She swallowed. "Of course I do."

"Not to me you don't."

"I don't really know you, do I?"

"We could change that."

5

Brooke blinked. Her belly swirled faster. Heat flared in her cheeks. *Why?*

She might not have had sex in two years, but she'd dated. Sort of. She wasn't afraid of men. Correction—she wasn't afraid of certain kinds of men. Mostly. Accountants, for instance. Those tended to be men without huge muscles or semi-automatic weapons strapped to their sides. She was wary but not terrified.

"H-how?" was the word that came out of her mouth, though she'd intended to say no.

"How do you usually get to know someone?"

"I, uh…"

He grinned and the swirlies whooshed into a tornado. "By talking. Asking questions. Maybe sharing a meal or a drink."

"You mean a date."

"A date. A conversation. Whatever you're comfortable with."

"I, um…"

He held up a hand. "Or you can say no thanks and I'll be on my way. No pressure."

The swirlies dipped in disappointment for a second. Her heart throbbed. "A conversation. Give me your number and I'll call you sometime."

"Give me yours and I'll call you now. You can capture it."

Brooke found herself rattling off her number before she could change her mind. A moment later, her phone rang where she'd laid it on the countertop. Then it stopped.

"Rodgers with a *D*," he said, winking at her. "Whenever you're ready."

He ambled back toward the great room. Before he disappeared, he turned and shot her a look filled with heat and humor. Brooke gulped in air. Pressed a hand to her belly. Cade was gone, and Grace was striding back down the hall.

"Oh my God, I hate all the peeing. And the morning sickness." Grace blinked. "What happened?"

Brooke tried to be cool. "What? Nothing. Cade came to get a beer. We talked. He left. No big deal."

Grace looked wary. "Watch him, Brooke. He's a good guy—they all are—but this life..." She shook her head. "I don't think getting involved with an operator is for you."

Brooke snorted. "Who said anything about getting involved with him?"

"You're right. I'm overreacting." Her expression brightened. "Want to see which room I plan to make into the nursery?"

Brooke shoved her drink away though she badly wanted to down it. "Of course I do. Lead on, Mrs. Spencer."

———

CADE WATCHED THE GAME, but his mind wasn't on it. No, his mind was back in that kitchen with the petite blonde sitting on the stool by the island. She'd been wearing a fitted olive-green shirt and faded jeans with spike-heeled boots. Her long hair tumbled down her back and her baby blues were captivating.

And then there were her tits. Big, beautiful tits that strained the buttons on her shirt. Not so much that the shirt gaped but enough that he kept wondering what would happen if they snapped off and exposed those pretty mounds.

His dick lifted its sleepy head, wondering what all the fuss was about. He forced it down again with an act of sheer will. *Not* getting a hard-on in the middle of this room filled with his teammates and their women.

He wanted to go back in there and talk to Brooke Sullivan, but she seemed as skittish as a newborn foal. After that moment at Mendez's wedding, Cade had been thinking about Brooke and why her friends were so protective. Grace had specifically said that Brooke wasn't ready for *this*. She hadn't said what *this* was, but Cade could guess.

Grace and Ice—Garrett "Iceman" Spencer—both had thought that Cade was only after sex. And maybe he was, but damn, he also wanted to talk to the girl. Because she was sexy and cute and he wanted to know her better.

Maybe it was a sign of impending age or something, but he was getting kind of tired of the singles game. Not that he wanted to get married or anything, but it might be nice to see someone he liked on a regular basis. He'd watched some of his teammates with their women, and he envied that easy camaraderie they seemed to have.

Brooke was part of this crowd. She understood how they lived. She'd also experienced firsthand what their job was when Alpha Squad rescued her because she'd been kidnapped by a group that wanted to trade her for Grace. That kind of knowledge was hard to come by. But it meant there would be no need to explain his life to her if they dated. No apologies for broken promises because he'd been shipped out on a mission. She would get it, and he'd make it up to her after.

Cade shook his head and stared at the television. What the hell was he doing anyway? Making up fantasies about a woman he didn't actually know? What did that say about him? She might be psycho for all he knew. Just because Grace liked her didn't mean the woman wasn't nuts.

He made himself wait until halftime to return to the kitchen. Everybody else had the same idea, and the kitchen was soon teeming with people piling snacks onto plates and laughing about one thing or another. It was loud and boisterous and fun.

Brooke had moved around the island, putting it between her and almost everyone else. Grace was at her side as they talked to Evie Girard and Annabelle Davidson. The other three women seemed relaxed and happy, but Brooke looked tense. She shot glances at the guys from time to time, and the corners of her mouth whitened with every instance.

She glanced over again, her gaze darting around the room—and then it stopped when it met his. His chest tightened for a second as her baby blues seemed to reflect fear. A moment later, she dropped her lashes. When she lifted them again, it was curiosity in her gaze.

He gave her a grin. He didn't think she'd respond at

first, but after a moment she grinned back. It didn't last long before she focused on the women she was talking to and didn't look at him again.

He headed back to the television with everyone else when it was time and settled in to enjoy the game. The third quarter was nearly over when his phone pinged. He glanced at the notifications. Shock smacked him between the eyes.

Brooke: *You enjoying the game?*

He quickly texted back. *It's all right. I'm a Cowboys fan myself.*

Dude! San Diego rules.

He snorted. *Seriously? Aren't they like in last place or something?*

Brooke: *What? No, they are not. Don't get all high and mighty. Dallas hasn't been so hot lately either.*

Nope, sure hasn't. He frowned for a moment. *Wouldn't this be easier in person? We're in the same house…*

Not for me. Can we keep it to text for now?

It was a little strange, but he'd go along with it if it got her talking to him. *Sure.*

Brooke: *I know it seems odd, but I'm more comfortable this way.*

You talked to me at the colonel's wedding last month.

Brooke: *I did, but in case you didn't notice, I was a bit drunk.*

So you had to be drunk to talk to me. Guess I should have put a bag over my head or something. ;)

Brooke: *Maybe this isn't a good idea…*

No, sorry, I was trying to be funny. You can text me anytime. I want to get to know you. There, he'd said it. He didn't know why, but it was the truth. Now how would she react? That was the kicker.

It took a few moments, but she finally replied. *Why? I'm a little weird, in case you couldn't tell.*

Maybe I like weird. But aside from that, I like your smile. Makes me want to know the woman behind it.

Brooke: *I have to go now. But thank you, that was sweet. I'll text you again sometime.*

Cade sighed as he put the phone down. Apparently he was becoming a pro at scaring Brooke Sullivan off. Maybe he just needed to let the idea of getting to know her die a quiet death, and move on…

Chapter 2

Brooke walked into the lobby of her building and waved at the security guard on duty. "Hi, Bert. How's Amy's ankle today?"

"The swelling's gone down and she isn't crying anymore." Bert shook his head. "Poor kid had a rough couple of days, but she's getting better. Her mama is babying her something fierce."

"I'm sure she is," Brooke said with a smile. "It's good to hear Amy is getting better though. I'm sure she'll be playing again in no time."

"She will. Thanks for your concern."

Brooke headed for the elevator. She didn't know Bert well, but she liked him. And she liked his wife and daughter too. They were a sweet family. "Tell Shelly and Amy hello for me."

"I will. Have a good evening, Miss Sullivan."

"Thanks, Bert. You too."

Brooke waved again as she stepped into the elevator.

When it closed, she sighed. She was typically an extro-vert, but she was so done with people for the day. All those big men in Grace's house. The yelling and laugh-ing. The sheer size of them and the way they filled a room. And every one of them capable of killing with his bare hands.

It was too much. It unnerved her.

She got off on her floor and headed down the hall, keys in hand. Max would be ready to go outside for a potty break. She tried to move quietly so Max didn't start barking. But you couldn't fool Max. He started barking just as she passed her neighbor's door.

Which of course meant the door opened and Scott stood there. He was tall and thin with wire-rimmed glasses and a chiseled jaw. A somewhat handsome nerd with a mop of brown curls who didn't make her flinch with his mere presence.

"Brooke."

"Hi, Scott."

His warm gaze skimmed her body. It didn't make her tingle the way she had when Cade Rodgers did the same thing earlier. She told herself that was a good thing. Scott was safe.

"I've got some lasagna in the oven if you want to have dinner in about an hour," he said.

"I've just come from a friend's house where I ate far too many football-party snacks. But thank you for asking."

He looked disappointed. "Oh, right. Well, stop by for some wine then. I haven't seen you in a few days."

"I've been working on a client account." She flipped

her keys. Max didn't stop barking. "I'm pretty tired, but maybe if I get a second wind, I'll knock on your door."

"It's been nearly two weeks since our last date."

"I know. I'm sorry. I've just been so busy. Thank you again for the flowers you sent."

"Pretty flowers for a pretty lady."

Brooke didn't know whether the blush of embarrassment she felt was for herself or for him and that corny line. "That's sweet of you to say." She turned her head to gaze down the hall. "I'd better let him out. He's going to have a fit if I don't."

"If you change your mind about dinner, just knock."

"I will." She stood there awkwardly, cursing herself inside for ever agreeing to go out with this man. He was truly sweet and she was a jerk for letting him think there was a chance they could have a relationship.

Oh, she'd thought when she'd first said yes to his invitation that maybe he was the one who could get her beyond this drought. He was a nice man. A safe man. An accountant at a manufacturing firm. Just the sort of non-threatening kind of guy she needed.

And yet he didn't do anything for her. The kiss he'd laid on her after that first date hadn't done a damned thing anywhere south of the border. In fact, it had made her want to run fast in the opposite direction. So what had she done instead? She'd said yes to another date. Like a fool.

Four dates in all and there was no spark. No response. At least Scott was gentle and hadn't tried to push her beyond a kiss, but she could tell he was starting to get frustrated with the lack of progression.

Before she could extract herself, he bent and planted a quick kiss on her cheek as if he had the right. As if they were a couple. It shocked her and annoyed her all at once.

"I'd love to see you tonight, Brooke. No expectations."

She pressed her fingers against her cheek. *No tingle. No sizzle. No spark.*

"I'll try," she said, though she cursed herself as she did so. Because why? She didn't want to try. She wanted to take Max out and then put on her jammies and cuddle up with Netflix and some *Doctor Who*.

"What time do you think?" Scott pressed.

"Um, around eight."

"Okay. I'll chill some pinot grigio."

"Okay."

Scott backed into his apartment, still smiling, and then closed the door. Brooke stood there for a moment longer before turning and hurrying to her own door. Dammit, why had she let him maneuver her into that? Why couldn't she just say no thanks and it's been great but I can't see you anymore, at least not romantically?

Because she had no spine, that's why. My God, she'd certainly told Grace how to handle Garrett back when he'd been her bestie's bodyguard, but she was no longer capable of taking her own advice.

With frustrated tears in her eyes, she inserted her key and unlocked the door. Eighty pounds of German shepherd waited for her with wagging tail and excited barks.

"Maxie! How's my baby?" Brooke exclaimed, dropping to her knees and hugging the squirming dog.

Max responded with a lick of her cheek. Brooke laughed. She'd never thought she was a dog person, but after the kidnapping she'd decided she needed a big dog to make her feel safe. She'd researched breeds and gone with a German shepherd because of their loyalty and reputation as good guard dogs.

They'd had some tough moments during potty training, but Max was the best decision she'd ever made.

Brooke grabbed his leash and snapped it on, then took him back down the elevator and out to the nearby dog park. After he did his business and she picked it up, she let him loose inside the area reserved for big dogs. It was empty at the moment, so it was permitted. Brooke took one of the Frisbees that lay nearby and threw it for him. Max bounded after it in a flash, and Brooke laughed at his enthusiasm.

They played for a long while, and then Max took off to explore the enclosure. Brooke's phone buzzed.

Scott: *I made a ganache for dessert. I know how much you love chocolate.*

Brooke sighed and huddled into the light jacket she wore. Her fingers hovered over the box to reply, but she ended up closing out the conversation as a wave of anger rolled through her. Why should she answer right this second? Why make him think she was hovering over her phone and waiting to hear from him?

The last conversation she'd had with someone was right under the one with Scott. Warmth glowed in her belly as she opened it up and perused it again. What had she been thinking to message Cade Rodgers in the first place?

Truthfully, she'd been smarting a bit from the tour of Grace's proposed nursery. Not because she wasn't happy for her friend but because she was beginning to wonder if she'd ever have a normal life again. She tried to imagine herself married with a baby on the way, and all that happened was that panic flooded her, twisting and turning and making her feel sick. What if something happened to her baby? What if someone tried to take him or her?

Before she could stop herself, she typed, *Did your Cowboys win today?*

She waited five minutes for a response. When nothing happened, she pocketed the phone, surprised to feel a wave of disappointment. She whistled for Max, then clipped on his leash and they went home.

She'd just set Max's food bowl down when her phone buzzed. She took it out, dreading that it was another message from Scott—but it was Cade.

They did. So did your guys, I see.

Now why was she glowing inside? *Win some, lose some.*

Cade: *So they tell me.*

Sorry I was so abrupt earlier. I just freaked a little.

Cade: *It's okay. I didn't mean to come on so strong.*

Her heart throbbed. What was she doing? Talking to this man, even via text, was opening herself up in a way she'd already discovered with Scott that she wasn't ready for. She thought of Cade earlier, his muscular body and soulful eyes, the way he looked at her, and that same pleasurable shiver she'd felt before skipped down her spine.

You didn't. It's me.

Cade: *I'm listening…*

I'm not all that relaxed with men like you. Men in your profession, I mean. Men who are as comfortable with weapons as they are with breathing. It unnerves me. There, I said it.

Brooke held her breath, but the thought bubble that appeared while he was typing reassured her. Because he was answering instead of just putting the phone down and backing away from the crazy.

Cade: *I wasn't on the team that rescued you, but I know about it. And I understand. But you know what, Brooke? I think, considering most of the men who were on the op were there today, which means it had to be on your mind when you looked at them, that you're pretty incredible.*

Her eyes filled with tears. She didn't feel incredible. If anything, she felt worthless and stupid for still dwelling on what had happened almost two years ago. She hadn't really been hurt, though she'd been threatened and she'd had a gun held to her head. She'd also been fondled and forcibly kissed, though she hadn't told anyone about that. Not even Grace. What good would it have done? Grace would have felt more guilty than she already did, and Garrett wouldn't have been much better. He'd been held with her for a while, and she knew that it killed him he hadn't been able to get her free sooner.

She'd put on a brave front in the aftermath of the incident, pretending everything was okay, being strong for Grace. But she hadn't been okay. The nightmares had only been the beginning of her descent into paranoia and fear.

But she *would* get right again. It just took time. She sniffled and swiped her eyes so she could see the phone.

I'm not but I'm trying.

Cade: *I hesitate to say this, but I'm gonna anyway. If you want to talk about it, I'm here.*

I appreciate that. I went to therapy for a while. I'm not sure talking more will help.

Cade: *Nevertheless, I'm here. I'm not a therapist, but I know what it feels like to be out there in the thick of it and to deal with the kind of people who kidnapped you. You can't shock me with any negative feelings you might have about them.*

Like I want them all to die? Stuff like that?

Cade: *That's right. Some people don't deserve to live. It's not my place to make that decision, but they often make it for themselves when they do bad things. If I'm sent after them, I'm going to finish the job.*

That right there is what makes me shiver, Cade. That attitude.

Cade: *I know. But I won't hide who I am from you. I'm Special Forces. I fight battles and I kill people when necessary. If I don't believe I'm doing something for the greater good, then what does that make me?*

Brooke shuddered. *I have to go now. Have a good evening.*

Cade: *You too.*

Brooke put the phone down and closed her eyes as she leaned back on the couch. Part of her wanted to keep texting him, and part of her said it was time to shut it down. Really, if she was smart, she wouldn't contact him again. In fact, she'd block his number.

But she wasn't all that smart apparently. Because she knew, without a doubt, that she'd text him again.

Chapter 3

The dinging of his phone woke him at midnight. Cade rolled over and grabbed the device, wondering if there was a recall at HQ or something.

But it wasn't that at all. It was a message from Brooke: *I can't sleep.*

He frowned as he pushed upright to sit against the headboard. *Me neither.*

It was a lie, but so what? She didn't have to know that.

Brooke: *I shouldn't have texted you this late. I'm sorry. But I figured you'd have your Do Not Disturb on and wouldn't answer if you were asleep. And if you were awake, well, maybe you'd talk to me.*

Talk for real or talk like this?

Brooke: *Like this for now.*

What did you want to talk about?

Brooke: *You said you understood. What those kinds of people were like, I mean. I don't think most do. My therapist— Well, she said that I had to learn to let go. That it would take time. But it's been almost two years, and I don't feel any more normal than I did after it happened.*

I can't fix it for you, Brooke. I don't know what to say. But I can tell you that being pissed for a very long time is perfectly normal to me. Hell, I'm still angry about some of the missions I've been on—some of the people who did terrible things to others. You don't just get over that.

Brooke: *You won't tell Garrett or Grace about this, will you? I mean about what I'm saying to you, not about us talking.*

He appreciated that she'd clarified that. Not that it would have made a difference in his answer. *Not if you don't want me to, no. Besides, I don't routinely share the contents of my private conversations with a gorgeous woman to my friends.*

Brooke: *Grace gets upset because she feels guilty about what happened. Because those men wanted her and her brain. I was just a bit of leverage—and disposable at that. If not for Garrett, I think they would have killed me.*

He hated that she carried that burden. *They would have killed you and Garrett both. And they would have killed Grace once they had what they wanted. You were no more disposable than they were.*

Brooke: *You think that's true?*

Absolutely. People like that only want power—everything else is secondary. Once they'd gotten what they wanted from Grace, she'd have been disposed of.

Brooke: *I still have nightmares sometimes. I'm in my house, in my bed, and I hear a noise. And then there's a hand on my mouth and I scream but nothing comes out. When I wake up, I'm in a room with a big, hulking man who speaks with a Russian accent. He is not nice.*

There was a long pause but the thought bubble was still flashing, so he waited.

Brooke: *I dream it, but that's what happened. They took me from my bed. I don't feel safe anymore.*

Cade wanted to break something. And then he wanted to hold her. Neither of those things was happening though.

I understand, but let's walk through this a bit. He was thinking of her physical security, thinking that if he could help her plug any holes there, she might feel a bit better. At least for a short time anyway. *You live in a house or an apartment?*

Brooke: *Apartment. I bought a condo and sold my house. I'm on the 8th floor.*

That's good. Means nobody's coming through a window.

He didn't tell her that he could do it. Hell, any of his guys could. With the right equipment and a plan, they could get into anywhere.

He continued, *You have an alarm system?*

Brooke: *The building has security, and I had an alarm installed on my door. I also have a dog. A big dog.*

That's all good. What about cameras?

Brooke: *No cameras. I should get some.*

If they make you feel better, yes. Sounds to me like you've got a pretty good system there. What kind of dog?

Brooke: *German shepherd. His name is Max. Really it's Max von Barkenstein, but we go with Max for short.*

Cade snorted. Max von Barkenstein. Cute. *Can't get a better guard dog. I'd say you're good to go. Nobody's surprising you in the middle of the night again.*

He didn't tell her that a determined foe could still get to her because she didn't need to hear that.

Brooke: *Thanks. I guess I still wake up in a panic sometimes, but I know it's not going to happen. Mostly.*

Do you feel safe right now?

Brooke: *I do. I'm in bed and Max is stretched out beside me. The windows are all shut, the balcony door is locked. The front door is dead-bolted. The reasonable part of me knows all this. But I still panic.*

Understandable. He thought for a minute, wondering if he should go in the direction he wanted to go or not. He'd either scare her or he'd get her mind off the things worrying her. *So you're in bed,* he began. *What are you wearing?*

He added a winky face and hoped she didn't take offense.

She sent back a laughing-so-hard-I'm-crying emoji. *What's next, Cade? A dick pic?*

He snorted. *No way. I don't send dick pics. It has to be seen in person to be believed.*

Oh my God, you did not just imply your dick is amazing, did you?

You said it, not me. He sent the wow emoji back.

She sent back an eggplant. He laughed. This girl was too fun.

You planning to tell me what you're wearing or not?

Brooke: *I'm wearing my Wonder Woman jammies. T-shirt, shorts, no bra. Very exciting.*

I could get excited about that. How short are the shorts?

Brooke: *Very.*

Don't suppose you'd send a selfie? He added the laughing emoji.

She didn't respond and he figured he'd scared her off. But then a picture came across his phone and his heart practically stopped. Her face wasn't in it, but there was a close-up shot of boobs stretching her shirt and little tiny shorts hiked up to the tops of her thighs. She was lying in bed, soft light spilling over her skin.

Cade's dick went from zero to sixty in a heartbeat.

WHAT IN THE heck was she doing?

Brooke's heart slammed against her ribs as heat flooded her. She'd just sent a picture of herself to Cade. A picture of her booty shorts and the strappy tank top that barely contained her breasts. Her double-D breasts.

Max watched her with that puppy head-tilt thing dogs did. Brooke groaned. "I know, Max. What was I thinking? I just sent a strange man a pic of me in my jammies."

Max made a noise and then put his head down on his paws.

Brooke started to fire off an apology, but the thought bubble appeared and she stopped typing.

Cade: *Think I need a cold shower now.*

I'm sorry. I shouldn't have sent that.

Cade: *The hell you shouldn't. I'm going to stare at this pic for the rest of the night. Might even make it my wallpaper.*

You wouldn't. She frowned. She didn't really know

24

that. He might. For all she knew, he was capable of anything.

Cade: *No, I won't. But I'm putting this pic in favorites. Unless you want me to delete it.*

Brooke blinked. *You would do that?*

Yeah, I would. It's private, and maybe you'd feel better if I committed your smoking-hot body to memory and did away with the evidence.

Oh wow, she liked this guy. It was sweet of him to ask. Her inner voice chastised her. *You don't know him, girl-friend. He could just be a smooth player and have no intentions of deleting. Should have thought of that before you sent it.*

"I did think of it," she muttered. Which was why her face wasn't anywhere in the photo.

She typed out a reply. *I appreciate you asking, but no, you keep it. My face isn't in it anyway. If you're the type to load it to your Instagram, nobody will know it's me.*

Cade: *Don't have Instagram. Or Facebook. Or any of them.*

Brooke's jaw dropped a little. *No social media at all?*

Nope. Not good in my line of work.

She hadn't thought of it, but of course it was true. Come to think of it, Garrett's Facebook page was pretty sparse. The last time he'd posted was about six months ago. So, yeah, some people weren't always glued to their phones or tablets.

I guess not, she typed. *But I have all those, so don't send me a pic you don't want plastered all over the internet.* She added a laughing emoji and pressed Send.

Then I'll be sure not to send you my [eggplant emoji], he responded.

Brooke laughed. She almost felt normal for a few

minutes, texting a hot guy in the middle of the night, exchanging cute little pictures and flirting.

I definitely won't send you my [cat emoji], she wrote. *That would be inappropriate.*

Cade: *Careful or I'll think you're coming on to me.*

Brooke bit her lip. *Would you like that?* She pressed Send before she could think too hard about it.

Cade: *I would. A lot. Keep talking to me, angel, and I may have to* [eggplant emoji][fist emoji].

Brooke's skin flamed. She'd never actually sexted with anyone—it had always seemed a bit silly—but she knew he'd just sent her the emojis for jerking off. Far from offending or disgusting her, it made her tingle. Not so silly after all.

Would you really? While we're texting?

Cade: *Not gonna lie that it's tempting. This pic is hot.* He sent five flames at the end of his message.

I don't have an equally hot pic of you, she typed. *Not fair.*

A few moments later, a photo of a bare abdomen —flat, toned, perfect—that gave way to a pristine white sheet covering his lower half pinged onto her phone.

"Holy cow," Brooke said. "Those are some gorgeous abs, Max. And whoa, that is an impressive bulge beneath that sheet."

Max didn't really care, but she had to tell someone. She was tempted to ask for a legit dick pic, but that would be taking things too far.

And this wasn't? Texting with a man she barely knew, flirting with him, sending eggplant emojis and photos of her body lying in her bed in pajamas?

"You aren't asking for a dick pic, Brooke," she muttered to herself.

Cade: *That work for you?*

Work? I think I fainted. And then, because she was already too deep into this, she sent several emojis. A cat, a flower, a taco, and water drops. She would have sent a tongue and an eggplant, but that was really going too far. Telling him she was wet was far different from telling him she wanted to lick his cock.

Cade: *You're killing me, angel. I want… Holy hell, what I want. Not saying it. Not even sending over a bunch of pics of it. Just picture my mouth. My fingers. Your sweet body and all the wonderful parts of it. Yeah, my eggplant is ready. So damned ready.*

She couldn't help but laugh. And shiver. The emojis were silly but safe. His words? Combustible.

I think this is crazy.

He wrote back. *So do I. But it's fun, isn't it?*

She lay still and felt the zipping of adrenaline and arousal through her veins. *Yes. Thank you, Cade. I think I can sleep now.*

Cade: *WTF? Sleep? And leave me like this?*

Brooke snorted when he sent over a wide-eyed emoji and the eggplant again. *Good night, Cade. I think you've got it from here.* She added the champagne bottle with the cork popping out and pressed Send.

Cade: *Nite, Brooke. Text me anytime. Especially if you want to discuss kitties and eggplants.*

Brooke plugged her phone in on the dresser and turned out the light. Max was snoring, but she lay there awake and stared at the glow of the lights coming in her window. It was quiet in her condo. Still. And lonely. So damn lonely.

Not that she'd had a steady relationship in the months before she'd been kidnapped, but she'd been more social. There had been sleepovers sometimes with men she liked. Not often, but enough that she hadn't felt totally deprived. Her last somewhat serious relationship, when she'd been younger and more naïve, had been over for nearly two years before the kidnapping. Which meant it'd been a long damn time since she'd had sex with any regularity.

She let her fingers trail down her body, beneath the covers, and over the cotton of her shorts. Her body gave off heat like a furnace. She wrestled with her thoughts for a few moments before slipping her hand beneath her shorts and into her slick heat.

Brooke groaned. She'd touched herself whenever the need arose, but this was the first time she pictured a man she actually knew. It didn't take long to rub herself into a shuddering release or to follow it up with a second orgasm.

But it wasn't as satisfying as it should have been. She went to sleep still longing for more.

Chapter 4

Cade woke at five a.m., blinking into the early-morning gloom, his conversation with Brooke foremost in his mind. What was she doing right now? Sleeping soundly, he hoped.

He'd jerked himself off after she'd said good night. Of course he had. There was no way after getting that picture of her luscious boobs, shapely thighs—and those bare legs that he wanted to feel wrapped around him— that he *wouldn't* bring himself to release. It would have been nice if she'd gone along for the ride, texting him more naughtiness and touching herself too, but he hadn't really expected it when they'd only just started talking.

Now he picked up his phone and opened it up to Brooke's photo. And, damn, he was hard again. He stroked his cock from root to tip, the excitement building until he reached a shuddering release that tingled all the way into his toes.

Holy hell, if it was that good just looking at her, how good would it be to be *in* her?

Cade got dressed in his regulation workout gear, grabbed his duffel, and headed out the door. He'd shower after working out at HOT HQ.

The mornings were getting chilly now that September had arrived, but it was still warm during the day. He threw his bag into the Toyota Tundra parked in the driveway. It was about twenty miles to work, and he took the back roads because he liked the scenery.

Five minutes after he pulled into the parking lot at work, he was inside the gym. Echo Squad teammates Sky "Hacker" Kelley, Jake "Harley" Ryan, and Malcolm "Mal" McCoy were there too. The others had either already been or they'd be there soon. He'd hoped to see Garrett Spencer from Alpha Squad so he could pry information about Brooke from him, but nobody from that squad was there.

"Where's Alpha?"

"Lockdown," Hacker said.

"That's right," Cade replied. "Forgot."

Lockdown was what happened right before they deployed on a mission. It's where they war-gamed the operation and went over plans. In the excitement with Brooke, Cade had forgotten all about Alpha getting ready to go.

He worked out hard, pushing himself to do even better, then showered and dressed in uniform before heading to his squad's section. Every squad within HOT had a section to themselves, though you could visit another squad's section by walking down the hall and popping in. There was an auditorium where they all met for commander's call when Mendez or Ghost gave an organizational briefing, and there were smaller conference rooms where each squad could work on a specific mission without interrupting another squad's planning.

Echo Squad had just returned from a mission two weeks ago, so they weren't necessarily on deck to deploy again immediately, though they would if they had to. Right now they had training to do, paperwork to catch up on, and other work to complete before the next mission.

Cade sat at his desk and pulled up a report. It was nine o'clock, and he wondered if Brooke was awake. He wished he could look at his phone and see if she'd texted again, but personal cell phones weren't allowed into the secure areas of HOT. Cameras and microphones could be turned on by enemy programs and used to spy on HOT's business. It was cloak-and-dagger stuff, sure, but it was also a real threat which was why nobody was ever allowed to bring in a personal phone, computer, or tablet. All it took was someone with good hacking skills and boom, they were in and national security was compromised.

"Hey, what'd you think of that hot little blonde at Ice's place yesterday?" Hacker asked.

Cade stiffened. Had he been that obvious? Or was Hacker simply being Hacker, renowned player and connoisseur of women? Cade had never known another computer guy who used his mad IT skills to seduce women the way Hacker did. He impressed them with what he could make a computer do, which Cade would have said wasn't something they'd be impressed with before he met Hacker.

Apparently there was something sexy about getting premium access to clubs and events with the touch of a button. Add in the fact the guy was a fully qualified Special Operator, complete with muscles and weaponry, and it seemed you had the recipe for a lady magnet.

"I think Ice would stomp you into a pile of jelly for looking twice at her. She's his wife's best friend."

"Yeah, but it might be worth it. That body... Man."

"Probably best not to go there, dude," Cade said. "Remember that Ice's wife is the president's daughter. You might find yourself locked in a dungeon or something if you upset her bestie."

Cade highly doubted that last part, but he supposed having the president's daughter pissed at you—and maybe the president by default because he loved his daughter—had to be a bad thing. Which also meant that *he* needed to be careful in how he went about talking to Brooke.

Hacker's eyes narrowed. "You interested in her?"

"Why would you ask that?"

"Because you're trying to dissuade me, dude."

Cade shrugged. "Just looking out for your best interests, man."

Hacker snorted. "Since when? Last time we were at a club, you delighted in watching some jerk-off try to kick my ass because I was talking to his girl."

"As fun as that was, that guy wasn't Iceman. Who, I am certain, would kill for his wife if she wanted him to."

"It's okay, Saint. You can just say you saw her first."

32

"Fine, I saw her first. And I already got her number, so back off."

Hacker laughed. "I don't know why you didn't just say that in the first place."

"Because it's none of your business."

"So you aren't afraid of Ice stomping you into jelly? Or of ending up in a dungeon somewhere?"

"Nope. Because I'm not trying to get into her panties, after which point I'd suddenly become unavailable and uncommunicative."

"Aw, man—is that who you think I am?"

Cade snorted. "Seriously? I've never seen you with the same date twice. I've also been around when you've had your face slapped while on a date by some chick you spent the night with. Remember the girl in Barcelona?"

Hacker winced. "Oooh, Maria? Yeah, that was epic... So you *don't* want to get into blondie's panties?"

Cade asked himself how he'd managed to get tangled up in this conversation in the first place. "Never said that. What I said was I'm not looking for a hookup and then never calling her again."

"Dude, you wanting picket fences and all that crap?"

Cade sighed. "Did I say that? Jesus, Hacker, there's more to life than fucking your brains out with a new woman every night."

Hacker blinked. "There is?"

Harley walked into the office just then with a goofy smile on his face, effectively putting an end to the conversation. Cade figured he must have been talking to his girl. Eva Gray was a tattoo artist that Harley had started seeing after he'd gone off on a special assignment to his old motorcycle club in Georgia. Now he was back with Eva in tow, and he'd never seemed happier.

Cade envied that happiness. He'd had relationships, but he'd never had one that made him feel like that. Usually his relationships ended with a sad fizzle, kinda like the air being let out of a balloon. Typically it was due to the life he led and the fact that no woman could seem to get used to being with a guy who routinely disappeared for weeks at a time and remained incommunicado for the duration.

"Man, you went home for lunch, didn't you?" Hacker said.

"It's not lunchtime," Harley replied.

"Then why are you smiling as if you've just gotten laid?"

"Because I was on the phone with the woman I love, asswipe. It's not always about getting laid."

"Whatever," Hacker grumbled, turning back to his computer. "There's something seriously wrong with you two."

Harley gave Cade a quizzical look.

Cade rolled his eyes. "Ignore him. He's just bitter because he went home alone last night."

"Because I wanted to," Hacker added over his shoulder.

Harley lifted an eyebrow. Cade shrugged. Mal came striding in, folders tucked under his arm. He held them out to Cade. "Present from the CO's secretary. Mendez wants them back by close of business today."

Cade took the stack and divided them up before handing a few out to the guys assembled. The others would be along soon and he'd spread the folders among them. "All right, let's get to work then."

"I'd rather be in the field than doing paperwork," Mal muttered as he took a seat.

"Wouldn't we all?" Hacker replied.

Cade didn't say anything as he flipped open the cover of the first folder on his desk. What he'd rather be doing was texting Brooke Sullivan. Or, better yet, exploring her naked body before spreading her legs and sinking into her slick heat.

———

DID YOU HAVE A GOOD DAY, angel?

Brooke smiled at the text when it popped up on her phone. She was working on a marketing plan for a client and feeling the pressure of doing it right, but a text from Cade changed everything.

Tension drained away as she picked up the phone and typed back. *Still working, but yes. So far, so good.*

Cade: *Where do you work?*

From home mostly. I have to meet with clients, but I make sure I'm done and home before dark. Usually. Right now I'm home.

Cade: *What kind of work?*

I'm a marketing consultant. I help you sell your product to the masses.

Cade: *Sounds interesting.*

It can be. It's not what I really want though. Brooke felt that pinch of sadness she always felt when she thought of the cute bakery she'd worked so hard for—and then given up when she could no longer manage to function the way she needed in order to run a business.

Cade: *What do you want?*

You, she thought. But she didn't type it. It was a shocking thought, especially since she'd only been texting with him for the past twenty-four hours. A few sexy emojis didn't change who he was. He was still a hard, tough man who did an impossible job. And she was still a girl who cringed around men like him.

I had a bakery. A little place that specialized in cupcakes. I had to give it up when I could no longer put in the hours.

There. Short and to the point. No tears, no whining. Just the truth.

Cade: *I'm sorry, angel.*

She liked that he called her angel. Though maybe he called all the women he talked to angel. She wasn't planning to ask because it made her feel kinda special. Besides, how did one ask a man if he commonly used endearments in his regular conversations with the opposite sex?

Thank you. It's okay. I'll get it back one day.

She routinely surfed real estate listings on the Eastern Shore of Maryland, looking for a quiet little town where she could open a bakery and tea shop. It wasn't going to happen anytime soon, but it was comforting to plan it.

Cade: *I like cupcakes. If you want to bake any. Keep in practice.*

She laughed. *Maybe I'll bake you some one day. If you're nice.*

Cade: *I'm always nice.*

Another text appeared on her screen, interrupting the warm feelings swirling in her chest. *Are you okay? Why aren't you answering the phone?* This from Scott. She'd known last night when she texted to tell him she wasn't feeling well and needed a rain check on drinks that he wouldn't let it go easily.

Brooke clicked over to the message box with Scott. *I'm okay. Just tired. I'm not really in the mood to talk to anyone.*

Scott: *I can bring you some chicken soup. Give you a back rub.*

I don't need soup, thanks. I'll call you when I'm feeling better.

A few seconds later, he replied. *Fine.*

Brooke knew with that one word that she'd pissed him off. But dammit, why did he insist on forcing her into agreeing to things she didn't want? Why couldn't he take no for an answer the first time?

She clicked back to Cade. And then, because she was feeling emotional and irritated, she typed out a quick message and hit Send. *If I told you I was tired and not in the mood to talk, would your response be to offer to bring me some chicken soup and give me a back rub?*

Cade: *?? That's a departure. But sure, I'll bite. No, I would not offer you chicken soup. Or a back rub, because what I'd really be saying is I hoped you'd have sex with me if I rubbed your back. Is there a reason you're asking me this?*

Brooke frowned. And then she thought, why not? Cade made her comfortable, even if it was only through text, and he didn't seem like a creep. His answer to her question was insightful. Of course she thought Scott was trying to initiate sex, but she'd felt guilty for thinking it because he'd never pushed her before and maybe he really did want to be helpful with the back rub offer.

I have a neighbor. We went out a couple of times. But there's no spark or sizzle. I keep turning down his invitations, but he won't take no for an answer. And sometimes I find myself saying yes just to end the conversation. So he wanted me to come for drinks last night and I said I'd think about it. But then he took it like I said yes and started making plans.

She took a deep breath and hit Send. Then she kept typing. *I texted later and told him I wasn't feeling well and wanted a rain check. So he immediately called me, but I didn't answer. And now he's texting again. I feel like a bitch for not answering his calls, but then I also feel like he just isn't taking the hint. It's frustrating.*

It took a few moments for his reply to return. *Have you told him in no uncertain terms that you aren't interested?*

Brooke blinked. Had she actually said those words? *I guess not. I should, shouldn't I?*

Cade: *You should. But Brooke, any guy who doesn't take no for an answer even to simple invitations, who keeps trying to make it into something more, and who calls and wants to give you back rubs, isn't entirely blameless. He knows what he's doing. And until you tell him it's not happening in direct terms, he's going to keep trying. And maybe even after that.*

That's what she was afraid of. *Would you take no for an answer? If I told you I didn't want to hear from you anymore, would you accept that?*

Cade: *As much as it would pain me, yeah, I would. Though I'd probably drunk text you a time or two and ask why.* He added a winky face.

I like you, Cade Rodgers with a D. *You make me laugh.*

He also made her horny, but she wasn't telling him that. Yet.

I like you too, Brooke Sullivan with an E. *You make me something too. Not saying what though.*

Brooke laughed again, then laughed even harder when he sent a picture of a devil with horns. Oh what the hell? She sent it back with a simple *Me too.*

Cade: *Maybe we can do something about that together. But only when you're ready.*

You mean via text, right?

Cade: *I mean however in the hell I can get you naked and pleasured. If it's via text, then so be it. But I think I can do a better job of it in person.*

Let's start with text. See what happens.

Cade: *Tonight? Bedtime?*

Brooke's heart hammered as she typed out a reply. *It's a date.*

Chapter 5

Cade drew his Glock and emptied the magazine into the targets that kept popping up as he traversed the course. When he was done, he holstered the weapon and walked back to the shooting bench. Brass casings littered the floor and the smell of gunpowder saturated the air. His team was cycling through the course one by one. Since he'd finished, he walked outside the range and pulled off the ear protection he'd been wearing. Then he took his phone from his pocket—the range wasn't inside a forbidden zone—and grinned when he saw the message from Brooke.

She'd sent him a selfie of her and Max. *The main man in my life. Sorry, Cade. I'm only using you for sex.*

He typed back, *Yeah, but I'm totally cool with being your sex toy.* He included an eggplant for good measure.

He rubbed a spot on his forehead and thought about the past week. He was dating a woman via text. A woman he'd spoken to only twice. He was also having sex with her, though it wasn't nearly as satisfying as it would have been in person.

Not that he minded jerking off to pictures of her tits in tiny tank tops or photos of her hand beneath her booty shorts. She'd never sent him a nudie pic, and he hadn't asked, but the ones she sent were probably more erotic.

She was unidentifiable, of course, and he approved of that. He sent pics to her as well, adhering to the standards she'd set. His abs, artfully wet from the shower. Hipbones—for some reason, women loved his hipbones. His happy trail. The bulge in his boxers.

She sent back emojis of tongues and water drops and hands, and all of it made him hotter than fuck. Jerking off with the emojis and dirty words flying wasn't a problem in the least.

Except that he wanted more. Much more. He knew he couldn't push her though. Each time he playfully mentioned taking it to the next level by including voices, she balked. And if she balked at that, she damn sure wasn't going to accept his physical presence.

It was definitely a problem, but one he told himself he was going to be patient over. Because he liked texting with her, even aside from the sex. Brooke was funny and interesting. He'd learned a lot about her in the past week.

She was born in California. She and Grace met in college and became besties. She'd taken a job in DC with a private think tank, transitioned into the political scene where she'd been a congressional staffer for a while, then left it all to open her bakery. She'd been doing really well, but then she'd been kidnapped and everything changed. She'd sold the business when it was clear she wasn't going to be able to keep up with it and gone into private consulting.

Brooke had an older brother and sister, and her parents were still married. Her childhood had been happy, she'd been popular in school, and life had been rosy. Which, to his mind, explained why she'd taken what had happened to her so hard. She wasn't accustomed to violence. She knew it existed, but she'd never experienced it. Until she had, which had traumatized her.

Brooke: *When do you get home from work, sex toy? I'm* [devil with horns] *just thinking about your* [eggplant].

Cade's balls tightened. *In a couple of hours. Stop making me hard, angel. I'm at work and the guys don't like it.*

She sent back the laughing with tears emoji. *Sorry. I'll behave.*

He sent her the hand emoji and a peach. *You want a spanking, bad girl?*

She returned water drops. A row of them. Cade thought his head would explode. This girl was killing him.

You like to be spanked? I wouldn't have guessed.

Brooke: *Haven't tried it, but it kinda sounds erotic. Especially with your hard* [eggplant] *in my* [cat].

Jesus, he was turning to stone. Serious stone. He wanted to fuck her so badly—in person, dammit. He wanted to touch her soft skin, kiss her, reveal her secrets to his gaze. He wanted to make her come while screaming his name.

Just so you know, he began, *I'm going to wear you down until we do all this for real. As long as it takes, angel. Because one of these days, I'm going to watch your face as you come and I'm gonna know it's my cock making it happen because it's gonna be deep inside you.*

He waited for the reply. The longer it took, the more he thought he might have gone too far. But then she answered.

I want that too. One day…

BROOKE SET her phone down and looked at Max, who was lying beside her desk. He'd been watching her with his sweet doggie eyes since she'd sort of whimpered at the last thing Cade had said.

God, sex. It had been so long. What would it be like to experience it again? With him? Would it be as good as her imagination made it every time they sexted? Or would he be one of those guys who only thought he knew what he was doing but in reality had no clue?

"Can you fall for a guy via text, Max?"

Because she really, really liked Cade Rodgers. Maybe he was nothing like what he seemed in their conversations, but she certainly hoped that wasn't so. He was serious and funny and sexy. He listened to her fears and then he had answers. Maybe not answers to fix it, but answers nonetheless. He didn't push her away or tell her to stop being silly or to get over it.

He asked questions. He spent hours texting with her. He was the first person she chatted with every morning and the last every night. And yes, she was beginning to long for more. Like hearing his voice. Maybe it was time to take that step.

But then she panicked, because what if they started talking for real and she didn't like him as much?

So every time she thought about telling him she wanted him to call her, she instead imagined all the ways it could go wrong—and then she pushed away the idea until the next day.

At which point she went through the whole damned cycle again.

Max tilted his head at the sound of her voice. She reached down and ruffled his fur, her fingers sliding through the soft silky mass.

"I definitely think you can," she told the dog. "I think you can fall for an idea that way, and I've certainly fallen for the idea of Cade Rodgers. Reality, however, is probably vastly different. No man can be so wonderful, right?"

Max predictably had no reply. Brooke sighed. "Back to work for a bit and then we'll do your *w-a-l-k*."

Max's tail thumped. She swore he was learning to spell.

Brooke spent another hour going over client accounts, writing marketing proposals, and trying not to think too much about texting Cade. When her phone rang, she was so deep into her thoughts that she shrieked a little. Quietly, but still.

It was the front desk in the lobby. "Brooke Sullivan," she said crisply.

"Miss Sullivan, you have a delivery. Signature required."

Brooke frowned. Since she didn't trust anyone, she told the man she'd be down to sign for it. Last thing she wanted was a delivery person at her door. She slipped on her shoes and headed down.

A courier with a package stood there, looking impatient. "You Brooke Sullivan?"

"Yes."

"ID?"

She produced her driver's license. The man handed her an electronic screen to sign and then gave her a box. She could tell by the sender name that the box contained samples she'd ordered for the fertility clinic marketing campaign. She refrained from rolling her eyes at the fact they'd wanted a signature and headed back upstairs.

When she stepped out of the elevator, Scott was in front of her door and Max was barking inside her condo. Scott was holding a bag. She would have darted back inside the elevator, but he saw her walk out. Inwardly, she groaned. Outwardly, she pasted on a smile. She hadn't seen him all week, but she'd texted him and told him plainly that she wasn't interested in a romantic relationship with him.

She'd gotten an auto-response that said he was traveling and would get back to her later. That night, he'd sent a brief *Okay. Thanks.*

So seeing him now was awkward, but not as awkward as it would have been if she hadn't finally been truthful with him. He glanced at the package in her hand and then back to her face.

"Hi, Scott. Did you have a good trip?"

He shrugged. "It was all right. I don't particularly like traveling."

She couldn't imagine. She'd always liked traveling—at least until two years ago when she'd started having trouble forcing herself to leave the house.

"Sorry to hear that."

He hefted the bag. "I was just returning the books you loaned me."

She took the bag from his hand. Inside were three books. Self-help books. When she'd first met him and he hadn't seemed to be hitting on her, she'd brought them to him when he'd complained about some things at work.

"I hope they helped."

He shrugged. "I don't know. Maybe. I might need them again, but not right now."

She waited for him to move out of the way, but he didn't. Her heart tripped a little faster. Being five-four and a hundred and twenty pounds didn't inspire confidence when facing a much bigger man. If he wanted to dominate you, he could. Even a tall, thin guy like Scott could overpower her easily.

She'd taken a self-defense class in the hopes it would make her feel better, but she cringed at the idea of using some of those techniques on a person. Though she would if she had to.

"I should really take Max out," she said.

Scott stepped out of the way. "Of course." But he

looked so gloomy that her heart slowed and sympathy kicked in.

"I'm sorry if I hurt you in any way," she said. "I didn't mean to."

He seemed surprised for a second. "I thought we had something special. You told me about the abduction, and I've never tried to push you to do anything you weren't ready to do. I don't know what I could have done differently."

Brooke wrestled with herself. Yes, she had told him she'd been abducted by some bad guys—but she hadn't told him what had happened or why. She'd told him the story in a particularly weak moment when he'd tried to make a move on her after they'd had dinner together one night. She'd used it as her reason for wanting to go slow, and he'd said he understood.

"I appreciate that you were patient. I really do. But I'm not the right person for you, Scott. You want a woman who can't wait to see you, who lights up when you walk into a room. That's not me."

"You don't know that. We never got beyond a couple of boring kisses to find out."

Brooke had an urge to punch him. But she told herself he was hurting and lashing out. "I don't think sex would change anything. Now, if you'll excuse me, Max really needs to get out."

Scott stomped down the hall and slammed his door as Brooke slipped inside her condo. Max whirled happily. Brooke leaned against the door and pulled in a few deep breaths. The confrontation hadn't been ugly, but it hadn't been pleasant either.

Max barked again sharply. "All right, all right." Brooke set the books and package on the entry table and took his leash off the hook by the door. "Let's go see what kind of sexy doggy ladies are waiting for you."

Brooke took Max to the park and spent time letting him run and play. There were some neighbors there with dogs that Max knew, so they all had fun running together. Brooke made polite small talk with the owners but kept her distance if at all possible.

After they'd been outside for about an hour, Brooke called Max over. He came obediently, and she praised him while she clipped on his leash so they could go home again. The sun was sinking in the sky, but it was still an hour or so until sunset.

Her phone rang. It was Grace.

"What's up, preggo?" Brooke asked.

Grace laughed. "Haven't heard from you in a few days. Just checking in."

Brooke bit her lip. Grace hadn't heard from her, other than a few texts here and there, because she'd been so busy texting with Cade. Not that she planned to tell Grace that. Her friend had already said that she didn't think Brooke could tolerate a relationship with a man like Cade. No need to go down that highway since it wasn't exactly a relationship.

Then what is it?

Brooke cleared her throat. "I've had a lot of work. Proposals and stuff. I got a fertility clinic this week. I've had to source sperm pens and cute little sperm stress balls."

"Sounds exciting. And a little bit naughty."

"I don't know about that. But it's been interesting. How have you been? Garrett back yet?"

Grace sighed. "No. He's been gone a little over a week. It could be another two or three weeks."

She hadn't thought about Cade going away yet, but she knew he would. And she'd be lonely without his texts. What would she do without talking to him every night? For the first time, she started to think about that. And she didn't like the way it made her feel.

"But you're okay?"

"Yes. Fine. Hey, I was wondering if you wanted to come over tonight. Have dinner. Watch a movie. You can bring Max."

She thought about it for a few seconds. And then, because she didn't want to have to explain why she didn't want to sit up and chat half the night but instead wanted to go to bed with her phone and her vibrator, Brooke told her best friend a tiny white lie. "I can't tonight. I have to work on the sperm account. I have a deadline to meet for a trade show."

Grace sighed. "Okay, I understand. It was short notice anyway. Maybe another night this week?"

"Definitely. Let's plan it."

They talked until Brooke reached her building and then they hung up with a promise to talk again tomorrow and make plans for their girls' night. Brooke waved to Bert, who was on the phone, and took Max into the elevator. When the doors opened on her floor, a man was striding toward the elevator. Max started to growl and the man stopped.

He wasn't tall, though he was taller than she was—

not that that was saying much—and dark-haired. He wore jeans and a dark jacket with a button-down shirt. Dark eyes glared at her and Max, and she found herself tightening her hold on the leash as Max's hackles lifted and he continued to growl.

But then the man smiled. "I am so sorry. I have spooked your dog."

He spoke with the slightest hint of an accent. She couldn't say from where, but she decided the language was Spanish.

"If you step back a few feet, I'll get him off the elevator so you can enter."

"Yes, that would be kind of you." He backed away and Brooke led Max out of the car. He didn't stop growling, but it was a low growl instead of an imminent attack growl. Brooke kept him on a tight leash as she pressed them toward the opposite wall from the man.

The man saluted her when she passed. "Thank you, lady." His jacket slipped open and she thought she caught the hint of a shoulder holster. But then he was inside the elevator and the doors were closing. He didn't take his eyes off her though and she shivered. The second the doors shut, relief flooded her.

Max had stopped growling and he looked up at her with liquid eyes.

"Good boy," she said, ruffling his fur. She didn't know why Max hadn't liked the guy and she didn't care. That man had given her the creeps.

As they passed Scott's door, Max started growling again. Then he barked and didn't stop. Brooke was shocked when he veered toward the door and started scratching on it and whimpering. Her heart jarred inside her chest and sweat broke out on her forehead and between her breasts. She didn't know why. All she knew was that Max was behaving oddly and it rattled her.

"Max," she scolded. "Stop."

But he didn't stop. He jumped up and hit the door—and the lock clicked as if it hadn't been firmly closed in the first place. The door swung wide. Max tugged her forward like a sled dog on the Iditarod, wheezing and barking.

It took her a moment to realize there was a body lying on the floor...

Brooke yanked on the leash before Max reached Scott's side. A red puddle flowed around his still body, and empty eyes stared glassily at the ceiling.

Brooke froze. A moment later, the floor rushed up to meet her and everything went black.

Chapter 6

It had been a long day at HOT HQ and Cade was just climbing into his truck when his phone rang. He looked at the display in shock. And then he punched the Accept button before it went to voice mail. If Brooke had finally worked up to speaking to him, he wasn't letting her leave a message.

There was also, in the back of his brain, the idea that if she was actually calling him, something was wrong.

"Hey," he said. "Everything okay?"

Her voice was barely a whisper. "No," she said. "I… Cade, I need help."

Every hackle on his body prickled to attention. His heart squeezed in his chest. His blood ran cold.

"What's wrong, angel? Tell me what you need. Where are you?"

She sniffed. *Tears.* "At the hospital. There's a policeman with me, but…"

His heart was a wild thing in his chest. "Brooke, baby, tell me which hospital. I'm coming."

She named the hospital and he fired up his truck. His phone synced with the truck so she was on speaker and he could drive.

"Can you tell me what happened? Are you hurt?"

"I'm okay."

"Ma'am," someone said in the background. "We're going to need a statement."

"I need to go, Cade. You're coming, right?"

He gripped the wheel hard. "I'm coming, angel. I'll be there as soon as I can."

CADE BROKE several speed limits to get to the hospital in Arlington, but finally he was striding into the ER and up to the desk. He was still in uniform, and the nurse behind the desk blinked a couple of times as she gazed up at him.

"I'm looking for Brooke Sullivan," he said.

The nurse blinked a few more times before reaching for her keyboard. "Are you family?"

"I'm a friend. The friend she called to come get her."

"Name?"

His last name was on his chest but he didn't bother pointing that out. "Cade Rodgers."

She stood. "I'll buzz you back. Room five."

He went over to the double doors and waited for them to open. Then he strode inside, past another desk with doctors and nurses, past medical equipment that beeped and whooshed, and over to room five. The door was closed. He knocked and then opened it when he heard her voice.

Brooke lay in a bed with a hospital gown covering her body, her face pale. When she saw him, she burst into tears.

For a moment he didn't know what to do. And then he went over and sank down on the chair beside the bed.

"Hey, what's this? You're gonna give a guy a complex, angel."

She covered her eyes with a hand. Her other hand lay in her lap. He took it gently in his. Her hand was cold, but she didn't jerk away. Instead, she gripped him tight. He let her cry.

A few moments later, she gulped in air and growled. "Dammit, stop it. This is ridiculous."

He plucked tissues off a stand nearby and pressed them into her hand. She took them and wiped her eyes.

"I'm sorry. I'm a mess."

"It's okay. Can you tell me what happened?"

She pulled in a breath and nodded. "I was bringing Max back from his walk. There was a strange man in the hall, but that doesn't mean anything because he could have been visiting anyone. Except I think he had a gun. But anyway, when we were passing my neighbor's door, Max went nuts. The door was closed but the lock hadn't clicked. Max knocked it open. Scott was dead. Bleeding out from a gunshot, or so the police told me. I fainted." She lifted a hand to the back of her head. "Got a bump on my head where I fell. Thankfully I landed on carpet and not the marble in the entry. No concussion, just a small knot."

Cade was trying to process it all. She'd found a gunshot victim and she'd fainted. She'd also potentially seen someone who might have done the deed. *Shit.*

"I couldn't call Grace. She would worry—and she's pregnant, though nobody knows it yet, but you understand why I couldn't call her and get her involved in this." She shrugged and her bottom lip trembled. "If Garrett were around, I might have called him. But you were the only one I could think of."

He squeezed her hand. "I'm the right choice, angel. You did the right thing."

She nodded. "The doctor said I should be able to go soon. I gave the police my statement and a description of the guy I saw. I'm not a suspect because they swabbed my skin and I haven't shot a gun recently. No traces of lead, or whatever it is they look for."

Cade's jaw was granite. She'd been at the scene of a murder and she'd possibly seen the killer. Even if they'd cleared her of actually firing the murder weapon, the police weren't done with her yet. Not by a long shot.

"Do you want to go back to your place? Or would you feel better somewhere else?"

"I have to go back. Max is there. Bert put him in my apartment for me."

"Bert?"

"Sorry, I'm not explaining well. One of the neighbors heard Max barking and called security. That would be Bert. He works the evening shift on the front desk.

He came up, found us, called the police and put Max away for me."

"Are there cameras in the building?"

She nodded. "Elevators, hallways, entrances."

"So whoever shot your neighbor is on camera." Thank God.

"Unless he's a vampire."

Cade hadn't expected her to make a joke. He laughed though, relieved that she could. If she could joke, she wasn't too traumatized.

Yet.

He frowned. Yep, *yet* was the operative word. Trauma wasn't always immediate, and she'd had a lot of it in her past. She hadn't told him anything beyond the first night when she'd texted him at midnight. That was as much as he knew about what had happened to her. That and the reports he'd read. They'd held her for about forty-eight hours. Threatened to kill her. Put a gun to her head.

Fucking Ian Black had been involved somehow. Cade didn't know precisely how because it was classified, but Black had been undercover during that op and pretending to be on the side of the bad guys. If Cade ever found out that Black had let them hurt Brooke, he'd kick the man's ass so thoroughly they'd be picking up pieces of him for days.

It'd be worth the trouble Cade would get into. He wouldn't even feel guilty for it in spite of the fact it was Black's help that had kept Mendez from being thrown in jail when he'd been relieved of duty a few months ago. Because of Ian Black, HOT had their commander and their teammates on Delta Squad back in one piece after the Russia adventure.

But if Black had let anyone hurt Brooke, it was all over but the crying. Nothing could redeem him if that was the case.

There was a knock on the door and a nurse entered. She flicked a glance at Cade and then focused on Brooke, smiling.

"I have your discharge papers. Just need to go over them with you, and then you can get dressed and go home."

Cade waited while she explained meds and dosages —for pain and nausea, if they happened—and gave instructions on rest and recuperation from the fall. Brooke signed the paperwork, and then the nurse was gone.

Brooke turned her baby blues on him with a tentative smile. "All that's left is clothing."

"Guess you want me to step out for that one, huh?"

She nodded. "Sorry."

He gave her a grin. "Not as sorry as I am."

"You've pretty much seen it all anyway."

"Not the parts I want to see. You always manage to artfully drape scraps of fabric over the good stuff."

Brooke laughed. Cade loved her laugh. He took it as a good sign that she was doing so instead of clamming up in front of him. They might know each other pretty well by now, but it was all through text. That had to make it a little weird for her. For him too. Mostly because he wasn't sure how familiar to act with her. They'd been intimate without being intimate. They'd exchanged all kinds of information. He thought that made them friends at least.

But what did Brooke think? She'd called him, but she'd already said he was the only one she could think to contact.

"Have to keep up the mystery so you don't move on to the next hot babe who sends you naughty texts."

"It's working. I'm on the hook."

She lifted her fingers and waved them at him. "Go. I want out of here."

"Yes, ma'am," he told her before stepping into the hall and trying not to think too hard about her flipping back the sheet and revealing her body in nothing but a bra and a tiny pair of panties. At least he hoped they were tiny.

He dragged a hand over his face and focused his gaze on the male at the nurse's station. Dudes didn't do it for him, so maybe watching that guy would get his mind off Brooke and her tiny panties.

But then the guy looked up from his paperwork, sensing someone watching him. A second later, he smiled and lifted an eyebrow. Cade nodded at him.

"Waiting for my girlfriend," he said. "She's getting dressed."

The guy didn't stop smiling. "Whatever you say, sir. Let me know if you need anything." He chewed the end of his pen for a second and then went back to his paperwork.

The door behind Cade opened and Brooke was there, looking cute in yoga pants and a jacket. "Did I hear you call me your girlfriend?"

"Yeah." Cade took her arm and steered her down the hall toward the double doors. "I think I accidentally hit on a dude."

Brooke snickered. "Accidentally? How do you accidentally do that?"

"Because I needed to think of something other than your smoking-hot body, so I was watching him instead. I think he took it as interest."

"I can give you a reference if you like. *Gives good text.* Something like that."

"No effing way, angel." He led her out of the hospital and into the parking garage. It was dark now, but the garage was well lit. She stopped walking before they'd gone too far. Cade stopped too. She gazed up at him with wide eyes.

"I… I'm sorry," she said. "I'm just a little overwhelmed."

"I know. It's okay, Brooke. You don't have to pretend with me. If you want to cry, cry. If you want to scream, do that too—only wait until nobody thinks I'm abducting you—" He realized what he was saying and choked it off. Her eyes went even wider. "I'm sorry. Poor choice of words."

She shook her head. "No, not at all. It's a normal thought to have. Somebody would think you were harming me if I screamed. I'm not planning to scream," she added with a little grin he wasn't entirely sure was genuine.

Hell, she made his chest squeeze. She was trying so damned hard to hold it together. Anybody who'd seen a gunshot victim for the first time would be shaken up, but someone who'd also been dealing with the kind of trauma she had in her past? Yeah, the woman was doing a pretty good job here.

"Do you want to go to Grace's? I can get Max for you."

"No. Absolutely not. She would worry, and I won't have that. Besides, Max might bite your face off. I wouldn't want that on my conscience."

"He wouldn't. Dogs love me."

"I guess we'll see." She closed her eyes and shook her head. "You sure you want to deal with my crazy? It's pretty spectacular."

"You aren't crazy, angel. You've suffered a traumatic event and you're processing it."

"Okay, we'll go with that."

Chapter 7

Brooke was out of sorts. Totally and completely. And not just because of Scott's murder. Though, yeah, that was pretty significant in her psyche at the moment. She'd fainted so quickly she didn't remember much beyond an impression of his body on the floor, eyes glassy and blood pooling beneath him.

If she'd gotten a really good look?

A hard shiver rolled over her. She didn't like to think about it.

But the other thing running through her mind and wreaking havoc was Cade. Specifically, his presence. She'd spent so much time on the phone with him, though not really on the phone with him, that he wasn't a stranger to her. And yet he *was*.

His voice was gravelly and deep, his eyes a shade of rainy gray she found amazing, and he was tall and built like a precision instrument—one designed for combat. None of those things came across in text, of course.

Though she'd met him more than once, she'd minimized his size and height in her mind until he was lean and not so tall.

Now she was dealing with the fact he was nothing like she'd pretended to herself. This man was big. Strong. More than capable of violence when called upon to fight.

And yet he was her closest friend right now, besides Grace. She asked herself how long that would last once he had to deal with her in person. Once he realized she wasn't the sexy, fun girl he sexted with on a regular basis.

Brooke's heart began to throb. Once he knew, would he move on to someone else?

Part of her had to admit she'd put off moving forward with him precisely because she was afraid that once he knew her better, he'd lose interest and want out. But now that she'd called him to her side, could she force him back into the box she'd put him in?

They reached a black Toyota Tundra that was sleek and shiny except for the TRD painted on the side of the bed. Cade held open the door and she climbed inside. Her head throbbed just a little, but it wasn't bad. The drugs were doing a good job of dulling the pain. In fact, as soon as she got her prescription, she'd take the really good stuff and go to sleep for a while.

Cade got in the other side and started the vehicle. "Where do you want to get those filled?"

She smoothed the paper on her leg. "There's a Walgreens a block from my place."

They got the prescriptions filled on the way and then Cade took them through a fast-food drive-through so they could get something to eat. Once they had their food, he drove the short distance to her building and, without prompting, shut off his vehicle. Brooke was both relieved and nervous about him going up with her.

They headed into the building, and Bert looked up with a concerned expression. "Miss Sullivan! Are you okay, ma'am?"

"I'm fine, Bert. Thank you." She turned to Cade. "This is my friend Cade."

Bert glanced at Cade's uniform. His eyes shone with respect. "Thank you for your service, Sergeant."

"My pleasure."

Bert nodded at his uniform. "Special Forces."

Cade smiled. "Yep. You a vet?"

"Four years in the Army."

Cade held out his hand and Bert took it. "Thank you for your service as well."

They spoke for a few more moments, and then Cade followed her to the elevator.

Once the doors were closed, she turned to him. "How did you know he was former military?"

"He knew my rank and he recognized my Special Forces patch. Usually requires some service to do that, though he could have been a military brat—someone whose parents were in, not a literal brat."

Brooke laughed. "I'm familiar with the term, actually. Learned it from Garrett."

They reached her floor. When the doors opened, her heart rate kicked up.

Cade was right beside her when they stepped out of the elevator. "I've got your six."

"Thanks."

She knew what that was because Grace had told her one time when they were going shopping for a rare toy for Brooke's niece. Grace had made the whole thing seem like a mission into enemy territory. Which, she supposed, it had been. They'd gotten the toy, but not without visiting a dozen stores and outwitting a few of their fellow shoppers.

There was crime-scene tape over Scott's door. A shot of adrenaline rocketed through her. She didn't know whether to scream or cry or shake uncontrollably, so she settled for hurrying by like something was going to jump out at her. When she reached her own door, she sucked in a breath as she fished in her jacket for her keycard.

Max started to bark as she laid the card against the electronic lock. Then the door opened and Max was there, whirling and wagging his tail. She prepared to grab him in case he went after Cade, but all he did was stop and tilt his head for a second. His eyes fastened on the fast-food bag that held their burgers.

There was no growling, thank God.

Cade held his hand out and Max sniffed it. Then he licked Cade's hand and tried to nuzzle the food bag. Cade lifted it out of the dog's reach.

"Sorry, buddy," he said.

"Come on, Maxie. He hasn't had his dinner," she said to Cade. She went over and got kibble for Max's bowl, then dropped it in and stood watching him while he dived in.

Cade had come inside and shut the door behind

him. He walked over to her kitchen island and deposited the food.

Brooke had been trying not to focus on being alone with this man, but it was getting harder to do. They were here, in her apartment where she'd given herself so many orgasms while thinking about him, and all she could think of was that she wanted it to happen for real while at the same time the idea terrified her.

Because what if it wasn't as good in person? What if he was terrible—or she was—and it all went wrong?

Max approved of him at least, and that was good. Though maybe Max had only approved of the food in his hands. Max had never growled at Scott, but he hadn't gone out of his way to be overly friendly toward him either. He'd certainly never licked Scott's hand.

And then he'd growled at that man earlier as if warning him. Brooke shivered. Max had known the guy was not a good guy.

"You want to eat now?" Cade asked.

Brooke gulped down her thoughts and insecurities. "Yes, please."

Cade started taking hamburgers and french fries from the bag.

Brooke went over to the fridge. She wanted wine, but that was a no-no with her drugs, so she grabbed water instead. "I have beer. Do you want one?"

"Water is fine."

She got one for him too, then joined him at the island. He should look out of place in her kitchen, but it was actually kind of nice having him there. She opened one of the pill bottles and popped a pill before taking a bite of her burger.

Cade was halfway through his already. Big man, big appetite.

And there went that little shiver of anticipation right into her lady bits. Because, all things being normal today and not sideways crazy nuts, she'd be going to bed with this man in a little while. Not literally *with* this man, but with his words and emojis and her vibrator, and she'd have had a screaming orgasm in no time.

She was getting wet and aroused. Brooke crossed her legs and tried to focus on the burger. Max ate some of his food and then came over to try for a fry. When nobody gave him anything, he went back to the food. Then he was back again. Ever hopeful, that dog.

"He's handsome," Cade said. "Just like his picture."

"He's a good boy. I don't know what I'd do without him. He keeps me sane." She knew Cade didn't have any pets. It was hard with his job to have one. Too difficult to arrange care every time he went away.

"He deserves a french fry for that."

"He's a scam artist. Don't let him convince you he needs one," she added when Max, sensing a soft target, turned his attention to Cade.

"Sorry, dude. Mama says you can't have one. Too bad because they sure are good. Mmm, good."

"You're terrible. Don't tease him." But she laughed.

"I'm not teasing him. I'm making you feel bad for refusing to let him have one."

"Fine. But just one. He'll never stop begging this way."

"And he just started today?" Cade asked, dropping a fry for Max, who vacuumed it up without hesitation. "I'm going to guess his mama hasn't been perfect when it comes to feeding him treats."

"No, I definitely haven't. Which is why I have to be more firm now."

She nibbled a french fry, hoping it might be more appealing than the burger, which she was having a hard time with. Not because she didn't like burgers—she definitely did—but the thought of Scott lying dead on the floor kept twisting her belly into knots. Finally she set the uneaten burger down and nibbled another fry. Cade's brows drew together.

"Something wrong with it?"

"No, it's me. I keep thinking about..."

"I know. But you have to eat something or those meds are going to kick your ass even worse than they already plan to."

She *was* feeling a little woozy. She picked up the wrapped burger again and took another bite. Cade smiled. She liked his smile. Brooke choked down that bite and then another before setting the half-eaten burger down again. She attacked the french fries. They were easier to eat.

"Thanks for coming to get me at the hospital."

"You're welcome."

"It's a lot to expect, I know that." She was starting to babble. But she didn't know what to say and it made her nervous. Which made her mouth work overtime. She opened it again to speak, but he cut her off.

"Brooke. Look at me."

She did, but it wasn't easy because her heart raced whenever she did.

"I like you. If we're nothing else to each other, we're friends, okay? You've been around me and my team-mates enough to know what we do for our friends."

Her palms were sweating. "I like you too. I want to be friends."

His stormy gray eyes were intense. "We are. The truth is I want to be more than friends... but I'll settle for friends for now."

SHE DROPPED her gaze again and fiddled with her french fries, swirling one in the ketchup packet she'd opened. He didn't push her because he knew it was hard for her. They'd gone from texting only to suddenly being in each other's presence, which was a big leap for Brooke.

He hadn't understood why she wouldn't transition to speaking on the phone, but he'd respected it. And now he was here in the same room with her, no doubt imposing and foreign—and probably somewhat embar-rassing considering all the things she'd said to him from the safety of her isolation.

He could picture all those texts, the sexual heat in them, though he firmly kept them locked away in his head right now. Thinking about it would only arouse him.

Slowly it occurred to him that maybe that was a problem for her too. The way she didn't look at him.

The way she kept crossing and uncrossing her legs. Cade sighed. Because there was nothing he could do about it. Not tonight when she was aching from her fall, taking meds, and probably dwelling on what she'd seen earlier. How could she not?

She continued to pick at her fries and he finished all his. It'd been a long day of training and paperwork at HOT HQ, so he felt justified in eating everything. He made small talk, nothing too difficult or about any topics that might be thorny ground for them, but Brooke's answers took longer and longer to come. Her meds were starting to kick in. When her eyelids began to droop, he figured it was time to get her to bed before she fell off the barstool.

"Why don't you go to bed, angel?"

She blinked at him. "I'm fine."

Cade stood. "You aren't fine, honey. You're fighting your meds. Come on, let's put you to bed."

She let him help her off the stool. And then she swayed into him and he caught her close. Her hair smelled like flowers and her skin was soft. She clutched his biceps to right herself.

"Sorry," she said.

"It's okay." He started to lead her down the hall, figuring it wouldn't take a genius to find the bedroom. And it didn't, because there were only two. One was clearly a guest room with a full-size bed and decorative furniture. There was nothing personal on the bedside table, so that's what made him think it wasn't her room.

The next room was larger, with a king-size bed and white linens. The walls were a soothing gray, and the lamps were sleek silver jobs. The curtains were pale blue with white sheers and the windows took up the entire wall. A television sat on a dresser against one wall, and there was a phone charger and several books on one nightstand. *Bingo.*

He tugged the covers back—because of course her bed was made—and gently sat her down on it. When he dropped to one knee to remove her shoes, she giggled softly and threaded her hands in his hair. His scalp tingled at her touch, and his dick started to throb.

"You're so pretty, Cade."

He tried not to laugh. Brooke Sullivan was clearly one of those people for whom pain meds gave her an instant high. If she remembered this when she woke up, she'd probably be horrified.

"So are you, angel," he said as he finished removing her shoes and looked up at her.

"It's been so long since I've had sex." She sighed. "So damned long."

Oh yeah, his cock was going to react to that news. No stopping it now.

"Who are you kidding? We had sex last night. Or did you forget?"

She sighed. "Real sex, Cade. The kind where I get to touch a real penis instead of a rubber one."

Oh sweet Jesus.

"I don't think you're up to it tonight, angel. How about you go to sleep and we'll talk about it in the morning?"

She looked panicky for a second. "You aren't leaving me, are you? I don't want to be alone."

"No, I'm not leaving you. I'll take Max out again, and I'll sleep in the guest room. All you gotta do is yell and I'll be here, okay?"

She nodded. He stood and pushed her back gently, lifting the covers. He didn't dare to undress her and put her into pajamas. He wouldn't survive it.

"My phone," she said, trying to sit up again.

"It's in the kitchen. I'll bring it in here and plug it in."

"Thank you."

He stood and gazed down at her.

She smiled and tugged the covers up to her chin. "You're a good guy, you know that?"

"I like to think so." He wasn't feeling all that good at the moment. He was feeling like a jerk for lusting over her when she was so out of it. If he were a different kind of guy, he'd take advantage of the way she was feeling right now. Because she wouldn't say no.

But of course he wouldn't do that. The thought that there really were men who would do precisely that pissed him the fuck off. Even if they'd been flirting this whole time via text, actually having sex was a different story. It required both parties to be cognizant and consenting.

Brooke closed her eyes and turned on her side. Her breath deepened and evened out, and he knew she was asleep. He didn't know how long she'd stay that way, but he wanted to get the dog out before she woke again.

And then he wanted to call Hacker and see what, if anything, the man could tell him about Brooke's neighbor. Because if anyone could find out all there was to know about a man in an hour's time, it would be Hacker.

Cade returned her phone to her room, then swiped her key and found Max's leash on a hook by the door along with a contraption that he recognized as a dog seat belt. Nothing but the best for Max. The dog whirled excitedly and Cade laughed. He was a handsome animal with lush fur and an intelligent expression.

"Sit," Cade said. Max sat. Cade clipped on the leash and headed out the door. He stopped to ask Bert where a good place to walk Max was.

"There's a dog park a block that way," the man said, pointing. "Miss Sullivan goes over there all the time."

"Thanks. Hey, who was the guy they found earlier? I know he was Brooke's neighbor, but I don't know his name."

He knew it was Scott, but not the last name. And he hadn't wanted to ask her and bring the incident to the front of her mind when he was trying to get her to push it to the back.

"Scott Lloyd. He was an accountant. Worked for Black Eagle Firearms."

Cade's senses prickled to life. The dude had worked for a weapons manufacturer? Didn't mean it had anything to do with his murder, but it was a lot more interesting than an accountant working for a clothing company or something. "How long did he live here?"

"About a year. He was a little weird if you ask me. Nice, but kind of off. He told me once that he was going to marry Miss Sullivan."

Cade hadn't expected that. "Really?"

"Yep. Not that he'd asked or she'd accepted—it was more that he thought she was hot and he decided she fit his plans. He had ideas about his life, how it was going to be. He kept saying he was coming into a fortune one day and that he needed a beautiful wife to be his hostess and the mother of his children." Bert shrugged. "Like I said, a little off."

"Yeah. Thanks."

Bert nodded to Max, who was sitting perfectly and watching them both. "To tell the truth, I'm glad she has this guy. I think Miss Sullivan needs someone to watch out for her."

Cade nodded. "Yep... and she's got me now too. Neither one of us is letting anyone hurt her—are we, Max?"

Max yipped and they both laughed.

"Sounds like a yes to me," Bert said.

Cade shook his hand. "I better get him out. Thanks again."

As soon as they were outside, Cade took out his phone and made a call to his team.

Chapter 8

Brooke came awake with a scream. It was dark, and she was disoriented for a second. But a cold nose shoved its way into her hand as Max made his presence known. He started licking her and she sat up, breathing hard and fumbling for her phone.

A bright light shone in her eyes. She covered her face with her arm as another scream formed in her throat.

"Brooke, what's wrong?"

She recognized that voice. She dropped her arm and he dropped the light. Then the light moved toward her. A moment later and her lamp flicked on. Cade hovered over her. The uniform was gone and in its place was a pair of athletic shorts.

No T-shirt. *Oh wow.*

"I…" She swallowed. "Bad dream. I'm sorry."

He shoved a hand through his hair. Max's tail

thumped on the bed. Cade reached over and scratched his fur and Max rolled onto his back. *Furry traitor.*

"It's to be expected. How do you feel?"

Brooke stopped letting her mind race over every damn topic and took stock. "My head hurts."

"Do you want another pain pill?"

"Not really, but I probably should."

"I'll get it."

She sat there while he disappeared for a few minutes. When he returned, he had the pill bottle and some water. He shook out the pill and handed her the water. It was ridiculous, but her eyes actually teared up a little.

Because she lived alone and she did these things for herself, so the simple act of someone else handing her a pill and water made her think of her mom and home. Sometimes it sucked living on the other side of the continent from her parents. If she were home, she could go to her old bedroom—still a bedroom, but not quite as personalized as it had been when she'd lived in it—and cuddle in bed while Mom brought food and pills and comfort.

She set the water on the bedside table and leaned against the pillows.

"You want to talk about it?" Cade asked.

She tried not to focus on anything but his face and eyes, but there was a lot of skin and a lot of muscle on display.

"Can you put on a shirt?"

He stared at her for a second and then snorted. "Got something against man chest, angel?"

"No," she grumbled. "But I want to touch it the more I look at it, and now is not the time."

Not when her head hurt and she felt groggy from the meds. It suddenly hit her that she must look like hell in addition to the rest of her issues, so she hastily smoothed her hair as he turned and walked away. He was gone only a few seconds before he returned, T-shirt covering his magnificent abs, athletic shorts still showing too much leg.

And too much male member, because there was no doubt something bulging under the fabric.

"Keep staring at it and you'll get a reaction," he said softly, and Brooke snapped her gaze to his as heat flooded her cheeks.

"Sorry." And then, because she had to do something, she made the mistake of continuing to talk. "I feel like I'm already intimately acquainted with it. I've touched myself so often while imagining—"

His gaze burned. "Maybe quit while you're ahead, angel."

She gulped. "Yes, I think so."

"So do you want to talk about your dream or go back to sleep?"

"Not about the dream. Just, maybe, talk."

"Okay." He sank onto the edge of the bed, just outside her reach. Max rolled over and Cade scratched his belly.

"I don't even know what time it is. How long have I been asleep?"

He glanced at his watch. Not a phone but a watch. She remembered that Garrett wore one too. All the spec ops guys did.

"It's two thirty."

"Wow."

"Either you were tired or those meds hit you like a ton of bricks. You usually react that way?"

"Pretty much. It's why I don't like to take them." She twisted the top of the sheet around a finger. "Thank you for staying tonight."

"No problem."

She felt like it was, actually. He had a job and he'd come straight to the hospital from that job. She didn't think he'd gone home while she slept either. So he had his uniform and what he was wearing now—and he probably had to go to work in the morning.

"What time do you have to be to work?"

"I took the day off. I'll be here with you."

Her heart thumped. "You didn't have to do that."

"Do you want me to call Grace?"

She shook her head.

"Then it has to be me. Who would take Max out while you're high on pain meds?"

"Bert could do it. Or one of the day guards. Jerry, Chuck—he's the new guy. You don't have to change your life around for me."

"It's okay. I have plenty of time to take. The military isn't the civilian world, okay? We don't get two weeks and that's it. I think I have about fifty-two days of leave on the books right now, and I earn more every month. A couple of days to help you out isn't hurting me. So long as you're okay with me being here, that is."

She was grateful and anxious all at once. Cade

Rodgers in her condo for the next couple of days? Helping her take care of Max, getting food and mail and, yes, keeping her safe from a strange man who had seen her get out of the elevator on the same floor that Scott lived.

Brooke shivered as she thought about the man she'd seen again. His eyes had been so cold. Didn't mean he'd been the one to kill Scott, of course. Perhaps he'd been visiting someone else on the eighth floor. There were four other condos besides hers and Scott's, and he could have been visiting any of them.

"I am, Cade. You're far nicer to me than I deserve," she added.

"We're friends, Brooke."

She couldn't help but smile even though she was a mess of nerves deep inside. *Cade Rodgers was here in her apartment. Cade! Her sex toy. The man who'd given her multiple orgasms through text.*

"I guess we are. Friends with benefits," she added.

"Yeah, not quite the benefits I'd like," he replied, grinning. "But we're getting there."

"It's strange for me, having you here. I feel like I know you and like we're strangers too. It's so odd."

"But you aren't scared of me."

It wasn't a question. She shook her head.

"That's good," he said. "I wasn't sure how you'd feel since we'd never worked up to actual phone conversations."

She dropped her gaze. "I know it's weird, but texting seemed safer. What if you didn't like talking to me? What if the fun we were having was ruined by conversation? And then there was the fact I made you smaller and less threatening in my mind."

She reached for his hand, stroked the back of it. He turned his palm over and she ran the pads of her fingers over it, a little shiver of excitement rolling up her arm and down her spine.

He didn't move beyond that, however, and she knew he did that for her. So he wouldn't scare her. A wave of emotion swelled inside her at that small gesture. Part of her wanted to fling herself at him, and part of her held back the way it always did.

"I'm not a threat to you, angel. Not now, not ever. When I gave you my number at Ice's that day, I'd hoped for the normal progression—a few calls, a date, some sex. But that's not the way it's going to work for us—and I'm fine with that."

She blinked back the hot tears that suddenly threatened. "I'm a mess, Cade. You don't want to deal with this. Hell, I don't want to deal with it—but I'm stuck. You aren't."

He tipped her chin up with his fingers. The shock of his touch—and of his eyes boring into hers—stopped her breath for a long, painful moment.

"You will never forget what happened to you, Brooke. And when you want to tell me everything, I'm ready to listen. Because I'm not stuck with you. I'm here because I'm your friend."

Her heart tripped and skipped along, tumbling over itself while her belly squeezed tight. "I've told you all there is to know."

His smile was sad and tender at once. "No, I don't

think you have. But it's okay. There's time." He stood and bent to kiss her on the forehead. "Go back to sleep, angel."

She wanted to protest, but she was suddenly too tired to do so. Her eyelids drooped—and she slept.

CADE TOOK Max for an early-morning run, then returned to Brooke's place and set about fixing breakfast. He turned on the Keurig, gave Max his food, reading the bag first to see how much the dog should be eating, then pulled out a carton of egg whites—of course—and a package of shredded low-fat cheese— another of course. There was ham (lean), which he chopped up, and then he set about fixing an egg-white omelet. He found bread, toasted it, and butter, which he slathered on generously.

He ate the whole thing at the kitchen island, then went to Brooke's bedroom to check on her. He'd fix her the same thing, but not until she woke on her own. He was just shutting the door again when she rolled over and pushed herself up on an elbow. Her hair was a wild mess as she squinted at him.

"Do I smell coffee?" Her voice was adorably scratchy and high-pitched.

"Yep. You want some?"

"Please."

"Cream or sugar?"

"Cream."

He went back to the kitchen and put a cup under the

Keurig, popped in a pod, and found the cream. After stirring in a healthy amount, he returned to her room to find her sitting up in bed, the television on with the sound muted. She'd smoothed her hair so it didn't stick up quite so much, and she smiled at him as he approached.

Max bounded in and jumped on the bed.

"Baby," Brooke exclaimed, ruffling his fur and hugging him tight when he put his face up to hers. "How's my doggie this morning?"

"He's good. Crapped a log. Pissed a river. Ate all his food."

Brooke kept ruffling him. "Did you do all those things? Were you good for Cade?"

Max licked her chin, and she lifted her face so he didn't get her mouth.

She laughed. "That's my boy!"

Cade thought he'd like to lick her mouth. *Not helpful.* He set the coffee on the bedside table. When she was done with Max, the dog flopped at her side, tongue lolling out, and she picked up the steaming cup to take a sip.

"Mmm," she said, eyes closing, and Cade told himself *not* to get hard. It was fucking coffee, for God's sake.

"You want an omelet?"

She blinked and stared up at him. "An omelet? Are you for real?"

He shrugged. "Of course. It's not hard. I live alone. It's learn how to cook a few things or eat takeout all the time."

"Maybe in a few minutes," she said.

"How are you feeling?"

"Much better. I think I'll have some bruising, but my head is mostly better." She lifted her fingers to touch the side of her head. "A little tender where I hit, but no more throbbing."

"That's good."

She bit her lip and sipped the coffee again, holding the mug with both hands. "If I'm honest, I can manage Max and take care of myself now. So you don't have to stay if you don't want to."

"Do you want me to go?"

She blinked at him. "I didn't say that."

"Then I'll stay for now. Until you're certain you feel up to taking Max out."

She nodded. And then her eyes widened and she reached for the remote, unmuting the television.

"The body of Scott Lloyd, an employee of Black Eagle Firearms, was found yesterday at his Alexandria address. He died from a gunshot wound to the chest. The police are looking for this man. He's wanted for questioning."

A police sketch of a man flashed on the screen while the anchor read off his description. Brooke's face grew pale.

"Oh my God, he'll know it was me. If that man is out there watching, he'll know it was me. I thought he might have been visiting someone else on the floor, but he wasn't, was he?"

Cade had gotten a copy of the police report from Hacker, who'd done some serious sleight-of-computer code, or whatever it was he did, to access it. *Male, five-six, medium build, dark hair, dark eyes, day's growth of beard, Spanish accent, wearing a suit with no tie, carrying a pistol in a shoulder holster, crooked front teeth...*

"No, I don't think he was. They've talked to all the residents on this floor by now and ascertained he wasn't here to see any of them. He could have gotten off on the wrong floor, so there's still a chance he wasn't the guy who shot Scott."

Though he didn't believe that for a second. Brooke had had the misfortune to run into the killer on her way back to her apartment. There was now, quite possibly, a target painted on her back. He was still waiting for more info from Hacker and his team, but he didn't think it was going to be good.

"I saw the killer, didn't I?" Brooke asked, her face utterly white.

"You probably did." Cade wasn't going to lie to her. "But it's not one hundred percent certain. That man could have been in the wrong place at the wrong time. He could have gotten off on the wrong floor."

Cade doubted it, but anything was possible.

"Am I in danger? Because I saw him?"

"Not with me here."

"But you won't always be here," she said softly.

"I'll be here as long as it takes, angel. And don't forget the security cameras. They'll provide footage of him, even if it's grainy. It's not only you who saw that man."

She nodded and then stared at the TV screen as the logo of Scott's employer flashed on the screen. "Black

Eagle Firearms? I honestly had no idea Scott worked for an arms manufacturer."

Now that was a surprise. Cade knew she'd dated her neighbor a couple of times. What had the man told her? "Where did you think he worked?"

"He said he worked for the Government Accountability Office. I thought he was going over federal spending for Congress."

"He did," Cade said. "He left that position for one with Black Eagle."

Brooke blinked at him. "How do you know that?"

"Because I have sources, Brooke. Scott Lloyd left the GAO over a year ago. He took the chief financial officer position at Black Eagle."

Hacker was digging into it right now, finding out what Lloyd had been responsible for, if he'd possibly gotten tangled up in any dirty dealings.

She looked thoughtful. "One of our neighbors had a cocktail party. It's where we first met. I remember I told him I hated the weapons industry and anyone who worked for it... It's no wonder he never told me the truth." She shook her head. "There'd been a mass shooting and I was having a bad moment, I admit it. But some of the guys there were going on about the second amendment and their right to own whatever they wanted and I blew. I may have said something about gun manufacturers being complicit in mass shootings. I was probably a little drunk—I also never got invited back to any cocktail parties there."

Yeah, he didn't think she would have been the life of the party among a group of people advocating gun rights. As a professional, he could see both sides of the issue. On the one hand, he thought weaponry was best left in the hands of people like him. On the other hand, people had the constitutional right to buy guns, and most people who did weren't crazed killers.

She gazed up at him. "I know you're carrying, Cade. I know it's what you do and who you are. But you've never hidden that from me."

"I am carrying, angel. It's like putting on pants. I just do it."

"You and Garrett," she said. Then she waved her hand. "All of you, really. Every one of those badasses that hang out at Garrett's place and watch football. There were probably more weapons in that room a couple of weeks ago than there are in a gun shop."

"Probably."

Brooke sighed. "I hate guns. I hate that people feel the need to carry them. I wish they would all go away."

"They won't. There are too many jobs that depend on manufacturing them, too many weapons already in the pipeline, and too many in the hands of law-abiding citizens and criminals alike. You can't get rid of them. They're here to stay."

"We'll have to disagree on that," she said primly.

"Have you ever shot a gun?"

"No."

"You should try it. It's not so scary when you get the right training. And it'd be another way to protect yourself. Max and a sweet little Sig Sauer P938—that's a compact nine mil. You'd be set with that."

She frowned. "I don't know. I'm not comfortable with the idea."

"If you ever want to learn, I'll teach you."

"I guess you're pretty good with a weapon, huh?"

He didn't let his mind wander to the innuendo side of that statement, though he really wanted to. "I'm an expert marksman, angel. I have to be. I can take out a target with my eyes closed if I have to."

She shook her head. "That's not possible."

"It is possible. We drill it until it's second nature. There's no room for *almost good enough* or *maybe next time* in battle."

She shuddered, and he thought maybe this topic had gone as far as it needed to. "You want that omelet or what?"

"Yes, please."

He turned to go.

"Cade?"

"Yeah, angel?"

"I said I hate guns. I don't hate you. I just… Some-times I think about what it is you do, and it scares me."

He gave her a smile. And then he told her the truth, because it was the only thing he could do. "It scares me sometimes too."

Chapter 9

Brooke took a quick shower while Cade went to fix her breakfast, then dressed in jeans and a long-sleeve fitted top that hugged her breasts and tapered down to her waist. It was a flattering outfit, and she chose it on purpose.

She wanted to feel good about herself, and she wanted to stop thinking about Scott and the man she'd seen in the hallway. It wasn't very likely, but she was determined to try.

She was still reeling from the fact Scott had worked for a firearms company and never told her. He knew she'd been abducted and threatened with a gun and he knew how she felt about them. That had to be why, of course, but it bothered her more than it probably should. He'd kept trying to move them forward in a relationship, but he'd hidden something pretty significant from her. Not that she would have expected him to quit a job or not take a job in the first place because of her. But she would have liked to have *known*.

Besides, it didn't bode well for a relationship if people weren't truthful. And he had not been truthful with her.

Oh, like you were truthful with him? Told him everything about your ordeal?

A flash of heat rolled through her. No, she hadn't told him everything, but that was different. She hadn't told anyone except a therapist—though she'd hadn't told Dr. Higgs *quite* everything either—and what good had that done her? She was still a mess and still dealing with nightmares and cold sweats from time to time.

And then there was that whole thing where she'd refused to speak to Cade on the phone because of her phobias. Now that he was here, she was a little angry with herself for keeping him at a distance the past couple of weeks. She'd liked him via text. She liked him even more in person.

He'd been just the person she needed to call last night. He'd taken charge and taken care of her, and while she'd still been scared, she realized it hadn't been nearly as bad as it would have been if she'd had to come home alone.

Brooke put the final touches on her makeup and then went into the kitchen where Cade was just finishing the food. She had to stop and admire his ass in his camouflage uniform pants for a long moment. He probably didn't have anything else to change into since he hadn't planned to stay overnight anywhere. The tan T-shirt he wore clung to his broad back, delineating muscles she hadn't known existed until that moment. His biceps bulged as he did something on the stove. He had some ink on his arms, just enough to be sexy as sin as his muscles rippled beneath the skin.

When he turned, he had a pan in one hand and a spatula in the other, and Brooke thought she might just be in heaven. He faltered for a second, his gaze going straight to her breasts and the deep vee of her top. She usually got mad when a guy looked at her boobs instead of her face, but she could forgive Cade because of all the naughty things they'd sexted to each other.

"Wow," he said as he slid the omelet onto a plate.

She sank onto a barstool and tried not to giggle and flip her hair. She failed. "So, are you a boob man?"

"You know I am, angel. How many pictures have you sent me of your cleavage? How many times have I asked for more?"

"A few."

"Yeah, a few." He set the pan in the sink and started buttering toast. Then he put two slices on her plate and refilled her coffee while she cut into the omelet. Oh, she could *so* get used to this. A hot, sexy man fixing breakfast for her?

Yes, please.

"Mmm, it's yummy," she said as she took a bite of the egg, cheese, and ham concoction.

"Good."

He did the dishes while she ate. Another point in his favor. She'd been afraid if she started talking to him for real that he somehow wouldn't be as wonderful as he was in text. She'd been wrong. So far he was the same man she'd grown to like over the past couple of weeks.

Funny, thoughtful, flirtatious, and alpha to his core. She'd wondered if that alpha quality would turn her off when push came to shove, but it hadn't. His take-charge attitude was precisely what she needed right now.

And then there was the fact he was just so hot. Like superhot with all those muscles and his dark hair and stormy eyes. He was pleasant to look at and he made her feel safe. Something which she was seriously in need of right now.

Scott's death had rattled her. The strange man she'd seen in the hallway had haunted her dreams last night, and now the media was putting his description out there. It frightened her, but she was also logical enough to realize a couple of things. First, he'd been captured on the security cameras the building used. And second, coming after her specifically made no sense in light of that fact. She didn't need to identify him because he would be identified on the video.

Her phone blared, making her jump. Grace's name was on the screen. If Grace had seen the news, then making her go to voice mail would only result in a visit, which Brooke did not want. She answered as sunnily as she could.

"Hi, Gracie."

"Oh my God, Brooke! I just heard on the news about your neighbor! Why didn't you call me?"

No way was Brooke telling her everything. "Why? There was nothing you could do. He's dead and they're looking for the person who did it."

"But his apartment! It happened *in* his apartment. Did you hear anything? See anything?"

Brooke made eye contact with Cade. He frowned but didn't say anything. She rolled her eyes to let him know she wasn't rattled by the conversation with her bestie.

"No," she fibbed. "I was out with Max when it happened, so I didn't hear anything. Didn't see anything either."

"Do you want me to come over? I can be there in half an hour."

"No, you don't have to do that. I'm fine."

"You could come here. Stay for a few days."

"Grace, I'm fine. I have Max. We're good."

"But honey, it was right next door. I know you're being brave, but this has to have brought up some bad feelings."

Brooke tamped down on the frustration and fear that began to boil inside her. "I'm fine, Grace. Really. Scott's murder has nothing to do with me."

She'd never actually told her friend she'd gone on a couple of dates with Scott. She hadn't wanted to get Grace's hopes up that she was turning a corner, so she'd kept it to herself. Good thing she had.

"I'm coming over. It's no problem. I can bring an overnight bag and stay for as long as you need."

Brooke loved her friend. She really did. Grace had been there for her for so long, but Grace was also working off her own guilt over what had happened two years ago, and she sometimes smothered Brooke as a result. Yes, Brooke had definitely had some bad moments and she'd leaned on her friend way too much.

But not this time. This time she wasn't letting Grace worry that she had a duty to charge in and fix everything. That she *owed* Brooke.

"No, please don't. I'm fine…" She met Cade's gaze. He'd folded his arms over his chest and stood there in silence. "I have someone with me. It's okay."

Grace didn't say anything for a long minute. "Who? Is it anyone I know? Do you have a boyfriend you haven't told me about?" That last was said jokingly, as if it couldn't possibly be true.

Brooke sighed. "It is someone you know. Cade Rodgers is with me, Grace. He's not going to let anything happen."

"Saint? You have Saint with you? Oh my God, are you dating him?"

His code name was Saint? She didn't think she'd caught that before. "Not really, no. We've talked on the phone a few times. We're friends."

"Oh sweetie, there is no way in hell that man—any of these alpha-male protector types, really—is capable of merely being friends. Be careful, okay?"

"I am careful, Gracie. Cade is here and you don't have to worry."

"I'll worry anyway."

"Don't. You know what he's capable of because you have Garrett."

"I'm not worried about his ability to protect you, Brooke. I'm worried about his motivation for doing so."

She didn't break eye contact with Cade. It was like

he gave her strength, and she needed it more than she realized. Hers had been missing for far too long.

"I'm not. Now stop worrying and let me make my own decisions, okay? Even if I crash and burn, it's time I started living again."

Grace sighed. "You know I love you. I'm here for you if you need me."

"I know it, bestie. I love you too."

———

BROOKE ENDED the call with Grace and set her phone on the island beside her plate. "Well, that went fabulously."

He recognized sarcasm when he heard it. "She mad?"

Brooke shook her head. "Not mad. Concerned." She tilted her head as she studied him. "Why do they call you Saint?"

He let out a breath. Of course that would have come up. "A few reasons. I'm not a serial dater like most of the guys. I don't chase tail when we're out at the bars together and then brag about getting laid. I call my mom regularly, and I also take calls from her even when it's inconvenient—and when I was a kid I wanted to be a priest."

Her eyes bugged out at that last one. It didn't surprise him because that's what usually happened when he mentioned it.

"A priest?"

"Yep. Don't worry, I've gotten over that notion. A little sin doesn't bother me at all these days."

She still looked surprised. No wonder, considering the things they'd texted to each other. Priests didn't have thoughts like that. Or shouldn't anyway.

"Wow, I wouldn't have thought that."

"Nobody ever does." He took her plate and set it in the sink. "I never knew my dad. My mom was a single mother, and she raised me and my sister the best she knew how. She worked two jobs and struggled for every scrap. The best part of our week was mass. I loved the pageantry and all the solemnity. Mostly I loved the look of peace on my mother's face when we were in church. So I thought that's what priests did, and I wanted to be one."

He'd been a pious kid for a few years, but like with most things, the luster wore off. He hardly ever got to mass these days. And when he did, it was usually when he went home to visit and took his mother to church.

"I just can't imagine how you went from wanting to be a priest to doing, well…" She was clearly struggling.

"To shooting people and blowing stuff up?"

She nibbled her lip. "Yes. One is a pacifist and the other isn't."

He thought about what he was going to say next. And then he decided what the fuck, he was just going to say it. "My mother worked hard to raise my sister and me, like I said. She cleaned houses, took odd jobs, whatever she had to do to keep the money coming in. One of those jobs was as a cashier at a twenty-four-hour convenience store. One night a man came in—drunk, high, doesn't matter which—and put a gun to her head. He told her he wanted all the money, and he wanted a piece of her while he was at it. He took the money and raped her."

Brooke gasped, and he wondered if he should have said anything at all. But it was too late now. He was all in.

"Do you know what Mom did? She endured it. The guy passed out and she called the cops. She didn't miss a day of work, just kept on going." His lungs filled with all the helpless anger he still felt when he thought of his mom going through that. "She kept going to church too, but it was somewhere around that time I realized prayer and sermons weren't going to protect me and mine unless I learned how to do it myself. So I did. Not that I knew what she'd really endured, because she didn't share that until years later, but I knew she'd been robbed and I knew I wouldn't let it happen ever again."

Her eyes glittered. "I'm sorry, Cade. Your poor mother."

"She would tell you herself not to feel sorry for her. To my eyes, she never spent a moment thinking about it after that night, but I know it's not true now that I've grown up. I know those late-night tears, the tipsy evenings where she drank a little too much wine, were a direct result of what happened. She pretended not to be affected, but it was a lie."

Yeah, he knew he was subtly pushing her with this story, but maybe she needed to hear it. Because Brooke wasn't telling the entire truth about what had happened to her either. Not that she'd been raped, but she'd certainly been abused somehow. She was balling all that stress up and trying to contain it, but one day she'd blow if she wasn't careful.

"She sounds amazing." Brooke dropped her gaze. "I should be more like her."

He put his fingers under her chin and tipped it up. "No. You're you, angel, and that's the only person you need to be. People process trauma differently. Mom's way was no better than yours. It still took a toll."

She shook her head angrily. "I've been letting what happened rule my life for two years now. I just want to be normal again." Her voice was barely more than a whisper. "And then yesterday happened, and I felt like I was being sucked down into the whirlpool again. Just one moment and boom, I was back in the nightmare. All because I took Max out for a walk at that specific time."

"I know. I'm sorry." He wanted to gather her in his arms but thought better of it. She might not welcome that much contact, and he didn't want to scare her. "But you shouldn't dwell on the timing. You can't change it. You also can't change someone's decision to kill. It happened—and if you'd been home, maybe you'd have heard the shot and come out of your apartment before the killer was gone. Then he might have killed you too."

Her face was pale. "You're right. I know you are. And I'm not letting fear win this time. I've got Max, and I've got you. That's a lot of badassery right there."

He grinned. "Sure is. We've got your six, angel."

"I appreciate that."

He loved that she knew what that was without asking. He returned to the sink to wash her breakfast dishes. What he really wanted was to keep touching her silky skin, but he didn't want to live in a state of perpetual arousal. Washing dishes was best. Except there weren't many, and he was left with nothing else to clean up.

"More coffee?"

"Yes, please," she said, and he refilled her cup, adding cream for her. "Thank you."

"You're welcome."

She took a sip. "You know, I thought it would be more uncomfortable to have you here... but it's really not."

"That's good. I'll stay as long as you need me to."

She smiled. "You can sext me from the guest room."

He snorted. "Not happening, angel. No eggplants and pussycats while I'm here. They don't compare to the real thing, and I'll know the real thing is a few feet away playing with herself while I tell her all the dirty stuff I want to do to her."

"You do have a dirty mind, Cade Rodgers with a *D*. I've gotten a few vicarious thrills from your texts."

"Baby, you have no idea how thrilling it could be if you'd let me do those things to you for real."

"I'm going to, Cade. Soon."

Chapter 10

Brooke's heart hammered against her ribs. Yes, she'd just committed to sex with this man. For real. But she wanted it, and she intended to get there as soon as possible with him. He did things to her insides that made her warm and tingly. He also made her feel safe and protected.

Would it all change if they had sex? Possibly, and that's what scared her. But, right now, the drive to be with him was strong. Shockingly strong, because while she'd missed sex over the past couple of years, she'd never actually had the desire to *do* it with anyone.

Until now. And oh my stars how she wanted it.

Cade grinned that sexy grin of his. "You just let me know when you're ready, angel. I'll take care of the rest."

There was something comforting about that idea. Letting him take charge and take control while all she had to do was feel. It was also frightening since the last time a man had been in charge, she'd had no say in what happened to her.

Tell him.

She bit the inside of her lip. Yes, she needed to tell him, but she wasn't quite ready for that yet. *Soon.* Her turmoil must have shown on her face because his expression grew serious.

"I mean that, Brooke. When you're ready. If that means an hour from now or a month from now, I'll still be waiting."

"And if it means a year from now?" Because she had to ask. Not that it was going to take a year, but what if Cade wasn't as serious as he pretended to be? Shouldn't she know that now?

He blew out a breath. "I'm not gonna lie. It won't be easy to wait a year—but if I have to, then I have to. Just don't shut me out now that we've progressed to actual conversations, okay? If you try to take this back to text only, that will be a big problem for me."

He made her heart wallow in warm fuzzy feelings. "I'm not taking you back to text, Cade. Though I can't promise never to send you a dirty emoji."

"I look forward to your dirty emojis, angel. Though not today."

"No, not today." Because she didn't think she could handle that either. Sexting him when he was in her condo? No way.

"You want to get out of here for a little while?"

Her heart thumped. "What do you have in mind?"

"I need a change of clothes. Thought we could ride over to my place so I could get some things."

She loved how he didn't push her to talk about her experience or to move forward faster than she was comfortable with. He told her about his mother, set it out there for her to examine, and then moved on. He was patient and calm, and he managed to gift some of that calm to her.

"Sounds like a plan." She had work to do, but she could get to it later. And maybe getting out for a while would be a good thing.

"You want to take Max?"

"That would be nice, if you don't mind."

"I don't or I wouldn't have asked."

Some people wouldn't want the dog hair in their car. But Cade didn't seem to care even though he had a big, beautiful truck with a black interior that was about to get haired up. Brooke sighed. Was it possible to fall in love with a man you hardly knew?

Stop being silly. It's lust.

Yes, it was definitely lust. But she also liked him a lot. Maybe she needed to be careful about that though. Because what if she started liking him too much and he didn't return the feelings? Sure, it was fun now, but it was still new. What about when it wasn't? Or when he got sick of her insecurities?

"How about we grab lunch while we're out? I know a place near the bay where we could take Max."

"That sounds amazing," she said.

"Then get your purse and your dog, angel. Let's get started on our fun-filled day."

TWO HOURS LATER, they were eating lunch at a little restaurant by the bay. They sat on the deck overlooking the water, and Max lay at Brooke's feet and watched the sailboats glide by. It was a warm day in spite of it being late September, and the sun shone down overhead. They sat at a table beneath an umbrella and ordered shrimp and crab cakes along with slaw and french fries.

The food was delicious, the setting perfect, and the company gorgeous. Brooke told stories about her marketing clients, laughing and using her hands to illustrate a point. Cade sipped his water and watched her. She was beautiful with her baby blues and her long blond hair. Her smile was infectious, and he found himself smiling more than he usually did. Because she made him want to.

Of course, there was a low-level humming in his veins, a spark and sizzle of attraction that wanted to roar into a flame—and would with the right incentive. He was mindful of what she'd said earlier, when she'd asked if he would wait a year to have sex with her. The question had shocked him and challenged him.

Because he wanted her now. He could wait, but how long? *How long?*

As long as it took was the answer that came back to him, especially sitting here with her now, listening to her talk about sperm stress balls and sperm pens and sperm mouse pads. She laughed about sourcing those things for a client, and he laughed with her.

A breeze blew in softly from the water, ruffling her blond hair. She tucked a stray piece behind her ear and stabbed her fork into her crab cake. She didn't miss a beat as she ate and talked and dealt with her hair.

He thought of all the guys in HOT who'd gotten married lately. Hell, even the colonel had tied the knot. Cade had always thought he wanted that, but he'd never found anyone he'd remotely want to spend that kind of time with.

And he couldn't say that Brooke was any different really, because they'd been together in person for less than twenty-four hours. But she was funny and sweet and vulnerable without being helpless. Brooke was anything but helpless, no matter what she thought.

She knew her foibles and she fought them. That was more than many people could claim. But she also sold herself short over them.

"Well, I think I've exhausted the topic of sperm. What do you have to talk about?" she asked.

Cade stole one of her french fries. "Nothing as interesting as sperm."

"But you're familiar with the topic."

"Intimately."

Brooke rolled her eyes. "I see what you did there. Niiiice, Cade Rodgers with a *D*." She nibbled a fry. "We've talked about a lot of stuff through text. But not everything. I'm assuming you don't have a girlfriend, though I don't actually know that."

"Do you really think if I had one, I'd be jerking off to your dirty texts?"

"Maybe. Some people are kinky that way."

"Yeah, and what did I tell her when I spent the night with you last night?"

"Mission planning," she shot back.

Cade shook his head. He had to give her points for that. "Good one, angel. Yeah, I could have done that. Hell, I could have a wife and six kids stashed away somewhere—but I don't. Too much trouble to try to sneak around."

She propped her chin on a hand and gazed at him. Damn, she was pretty. "I believe you. Just had to tease you a little bit." She sighed. "Okay, that's not completely true. The truth is it's something I'm a little paranoid about. I dated a guy for eight months and I thought we were getting serious, but it turned out he really did have a wife and kid stashed away. He spent the week working in DC and took the train to New York every weekend. He told me he was spending time with his elderly parents, but of course he was going home to his wife."

Cade wanted to punch the guy for her. "How did you find out?"

She frowned. "His wife came to DC to surprise him one day. She'd left the kid with his parents, who weren't all that elderly, and taken the train down. I answered his apartment door while wearing his shirt. We'd ordered food, you see…"

"Ouch."

She nodded. "Yep, it was awkward. She lost it, of course. Surprisingly, she didn't seem all that pissed at me. It was him she took her fury out on. So, yeah, I locked myself in the bathroom, threw on my clothes, and got the hell out." She gave him a look. "I didn't really think you had someone, by the way. Grace would have told me. I guess I sometimes still feel pretty ashamed about what happened. I could have just told you without the drama, right?"

He reached for her hand across the table and squeezed softly. "You told me, angel. That's all that matters."

She squeezed his hand in return. "I'm full of drama and weirdness, Cade. You should really rethink this whole thing. Even when I try to be normal, drama finds me. I attract it like a magnet."

He didn't believe shit like that for a second. But she clearly did. "I've thought about you a lot. And I'm right where I want to be."

She still didn't try to extract her hand. Her touch was electric, singing through him like a living current. He could only imagine how good it would be if they were pressed together with nothing between them but skin.

"You're too good to be true," she said. "Do you know that?"

"No, I'm not. I'm just really, really patient when I want something. And I definitely want you."

Her pretty features clouded. "I'm nothing special, Cade. You'll be disappointed if you think so."

"Why don't you let me be the judge of that?"

She shrugged and dropped her lashes over her eyes. "Well, don't say I didn't tell you when the time comes."

"You know what I think, Brooke?"

She lifted her head. "What?"

"I think you're full of shit."

He didn't expect her to crack up, but she did. "You don't mince words, do you? You just tell it like it is."

"For the most part." He leaned toward her. Her eyes widened just a little. Her gaze dropped to his mouth. *Excellent.* "Here are some words for you, angel. Take note… You and I are going to be epic together. Fucking epic. You think your vibrator is any match for my tongue and cock? You're gonna find out what you've been missing, and you're gonna kick yourself for waiting so long. Trust me."

He watched the flush crawl up her throat. "You…" She cleared her throat, and he could tell she was thinking about it. In detail. "You're awfully sure of yourself, aren't you?"

"Satisfaction guaranteed, angel. Think about it."

He waved the waitress over and asked for the check. Brooke stared at him the entire time. The wheels were turning. That was enough.

CADE PAID for their meal even though she tried to whip out her credit card first. She thanked him, and he came to pull her chair out for her. Max got to his feet, tail wagging, and they set off for the parking lot.

Except, when they got outside the restaurant, Cade didn't head for his truck. Instead, he started toward a path that went along the bay. "Let's take Max for a stroll. Unless you don't want to."

"No, that sounds good." She let out Max's retractable leash and he ranged ahead of them, sniffing grass and peeing on everything he could find. She should make him heel, but he was having too much fun —and so was she—so she let him keep going.

The water rippled with the breeze, sparkling in the sunshine. Sailboats plied the bay, schooners and skip-jacks looking like something from a postcard as they moved along. There was a lighthouse in the distance, an old Chesapeake Bay structure with a squat silhouette. Not at all like what you normally thought of when you thought of lighthouses.

People jogged along the path with some regularity. They also encountered couples strolling with babies and many others walking their dogs.

"I like it here," Brooke said as the breeze ruffled her hair. She'd never considered moving this far from the action of DC, but maybe she should have. Except for those days when she needed to meet with clients in the city, and then traffic would be a total bitch.

"I don't live too far from here," Cade said.

Brooke stopped and faced him. "Really? Wow, isn't this a distance from work?"

"About twenty miles. I like to get away from it all when I'm done for the day. And when we get home from a mission, I like to be removed from the job as much as possible."

The day was pleasant, non-threatening, which had to account for why she blurted out her question the way she did.

"Are you ever scared?"

He frowned. "You mean when I'm on a mission?"

She nodded.

"Yes. And no." He shrugged. "It's always there, in

your mind, that this could be it. But you can't dwell on it because you're the best-equipped, best-trained mother-fuckers out there. You kick ass, get the job done, and win. There's no room for fear because that shit will mess you up. But of course it's there, in the back of your brain. You just wall it off from what you need to do and get busy doing it."

"You make it sound so easy." She wished she knew how to wall off the fear. If she could do that, she'd have it made.

"Angel, I've trained for a long time. Hard training. You can't do what I do and get emotional about it."

Brooke swallowed. A cloud drifted over the sun, making everything a little darker. A little cooler. It brought back to her, forcefully, what he did when he went on a mission. There was violence. Men who killed. And women. She thought of Victoria Brandon, who she knew was a sniper, and her blood ran cold. How could Victoria do that? How could she pull the trigger, knowing the person on the other end would die?

But they all did it. Victoria, Garrett, Cade. All of them. Grace didn't seem to have trouble with it. Didn't even dwell on it other than worrying about Garrett when he was on a mission.

"Can you teach me how to wall it off?" she asked.

He gave her a sad smile. "You don't need to do that yet, Brooke. You need to deal with it first and then you can learn to wall it off."

Annoyance slid through her. "I've been dealing with it for two years," she snapped. "I think I can be the judge of when I'm finished, thanks."

He held up both hands, and guilt sliced her soul. "Whatever you want, angel. I'm not trying to tell you what to do. Just telling you what I observe."

The sun emerged from behind the cloud, but the mood was ruined. No amount of sunshine was bringing it back right now.

"Can we get going? I need to work on a couple of proposals when I get home."

His gaze was solemn, as if he was disappointed in her. It made her both angry and guilty at the same time. Why was she taking her insecurities out on him? And why was he pushing her when he knew she was having trouble?

"Whatever you want, Brooke. You're calling the shots here, not me."

She got the feeling he wasn't just talking about their day out. He was talking about everything between them. Somehow that wasn't a comfortable thought at all. Because if anyone was going to mess it all up, it would be her.

Chapter 11

"You coming in or waiting here?" Cade asked when they reached his house. It was a brick ranch on a quiet street tucked away in a small town. Not what she'd expected, because it looked more like a house that should belong to a 1950s-era family than a Special Ops warrior.

She expected an avocado stove and shag carpeting on the interior. "I'm coming."

Cade shut off the truck and got out. Brooke followed suit, Max tagging along behind her. Cade inserted a key in the lock and the door swung open. There was a high-pitched tone that blared for a few seconds before Cade punched in his alarm code and turned it off.

He held the door for her and Max, then followed behind and shut the door. They were in the small kitchen, and the stove was indeed avocado. The counter-tops were laminate or something because they were peeling up on one edge. The fridge was a massive white monster, and there was a coffee maker on the counter.

The flooring was vinyl and the carpet, when they reached the living room, was not shag after all. It was much newer.

"Home sweet home," Cade said, spreading his arms.

"It's cute."

"Tiny." He went over to the front door, opened it, and pulled mail from the box outside. "Junk," he said, tossing it after he'd scanned every envelope.

"Are you buying this place or renting?"

"Renting. You can't buy a house this close to the water, no matter how dilapidated, for anything I could possibly afford. But the rent is cheap because the lady who owns it is old and in a nursing home. She could charge more but she doesn't because she has no intention of leaving those bloodsucking leeches in her family a damn dime. Her words, not mine."

Brooke blinked. "Glad you clarified that."

Cade grinned and her heart turned over. "I love that old lady, let me tell you. She'd sell me the house except she's got it in trust to her favorite charity."

"Let me guess... cat rescue."

"Nope, not even close. Literacy."

"Oh, I like that," Brooke said.

"Yep, classy old gal. Her heart is in the right place. When she goes, they'll sell this place for a mint. Someone will knock it down and build a modern retreat. And a whole lot of adults and children will get the gift of reading."

Brooke's chest was tight. There were still good people in this world, that's for sure.

"Just give me a few minutes," Cade said. "The yard is fenced if you want to let Max out."

He disappeared down a small hallway, and Brooke walked over to the sliding glass door and unlocked it. Max followed obediently. She blinked at the size of the yard. It was much bigger than she'd thought it would be.

"Okay, buddy, you can run here," she said, unclipping Max's leash. He immediately took off after a squirrel that sat motionless for a split second before bounding away and up a tree. Max jumped and barked at the bottom of the tree for a few moments, then raced off to bark at another squirrel that ran along the top of the fence.

Brooke went back inside while Max played. She had an insane curiosity to see how Cade lived. The house was small, but of course there was a massive television sitting on a console in the living room. There was a couch with reclining seats and two end tables with lamps. On one end table was a stack of magazines. The top one was about guns, and Brooke shivered. She went through the stack quickly—guns, hunting, fishing, and cars. Typical guy stuff, she supposed.

There was only one photograph sitting in a frame. A smiling woman stood behind two kids. There was water in the background, and all three of them wore swimsuits. The sun shone down on their heads. The boy was taller than the girl, and he grinned a big gap-toothed grin. The girl looked shy.

"That's me and Mom and my sister," Cade said, and

Brooke jumped at the sound of his voice as she spun to face him. He'd put on faded jeans and a black T-shirt, and her heart squeezed tight.

"You look like you were having fun," she said, glancing down at the picture.

"We were. Mom worked a lot, so we didn't get days like that one often." He came over and gazed down at the photo still in her hands. "I was eight. Sissy was six. Mom would have been twenty-six then."

"She's pretty." Brooke thought of the woman who'd been robbed and raped and had a hard time reconciling her with this woman. She didn't look like someone who could have withstood that. But clearly she had.

"Yeah, she was. Still is. People always think she's my sister these days."

"I'm sure that doesn't bother her in the least."

He grinned. "No, not really."

Brooke set the photo down and pulled in a breath before she faced him. "I'm sorry for being bitchy to you earlier. You've been nothing but good to me, and you don't deserve that."

"It's okay, angel. We're still learning each other. It's bound to happen."

She shook her head. "Why are you so forgiving, Cade? Why do you keep putting up with me? You're seriously, ridiculously gorgeous. You can do better than hanging out and waiting for me to get my shit together."

He took her by the shoulders, softly but firmly. She didn't want to pull away, which was a rather shocking reaction in some respects. No, what she wanted was to close the distance between them and press her body to his. Then she wanted him to hold her.

"Get this into your pretty head, angel. I like you. I'm interested in you and in being with you. Could I walk into Buddy's Bar and pick up a hot chick tonight? Sure I could. I could pick her up, take her home, and spend the night doing all the things I've texted to you. But I don't want to. I want to do those things with you, Brooke. You."

Tears pricked the backs of her eyelids. The things this man said. The way he made her feel. It was terrifying and exhilarating all at once. "Why, Cade? That's what I don't understand."

"Honestly?"

She nodded.

"I don't understand it either. I have no idea why, but I know it's what I feel in here." He put his fist over his chest. "Something in here says you're worth the risk."

No one had ever said anything so beautiful to her. Even Gavin, the man she'd dated for eight months and thought she might marry before she realized he was already married, had never said anything so amazing.

"I'm afraid," she said. "Afraid it won't work, afraid of who you are, afraid of what you do. Everything in my head tells me not to let you in—but my heart won't listen. I feel like I'm on a train that's speeding toward a cliff. And I can't jump off."

He pulled her in close and put his arms around her. The contact shocked her senses, but she wrapped her arms around him and held on, squeezing her eyes closed as she focused on what it felt like to just be for a few moments. Without fear, without the past or the future clogging up her soul and turning everything dark and treacherous.

"So we'll go over the edge together," he said, his breath against her hair. "We'll sail over the side of the cliff and find out whether we crash and burn—or whether we fly."

HE DIDN'T KNOW what this woman was doing to him, but he was as helpless to fight it as she was. Cade held her close, wishing like hell he could tilt her chin back and kiss her but unwilling to make that move when just pulling her into his arms had been a big step. She'd stiffened at first but had relaxed quickly. When she'd put her arms around him, he'd felt like he'd coaxed a baby bird into his hand.

"I was assaulted," she said into his chest, and his heart turned to stone. Rage cascaded over him like a waterfall of ice.

"Angel," he said, because it was all he could manage without fucking losing his mind.

"They didn't rape me. But the man who took me from my bed that night—he touched me. My breasts, my... my..." She sniffled, and he wanted to kill someone. "He touched me inappropriately. Shoved his hands beneath my pajama pants and into me. He would have raped me if he'd gotten the chance, but he didn't."

Horror tapped a drumbeat in his brain. He had to

work to make his voice come out normal. "He did, angel. He forced his fingers into you—that's rape."

"But it's not what everyone thinks of as rape. I keep telling myself I wasn't raped because he didn't have intercourse with me. He stuck his fingers inside me, but it didn't last long. How can that be rape?"

Cade was ready to hunt down the bastard who'd done that to her. If he was still in federal custody, and he probably was since he'd been involved in a kidnapping plot, Cade was prepared to find him and kill him in his prison cell.

Except he couldn't because that would be a crime. *Motherfucker.* Sometimes being one of the good guys sucked.

"It is, Brooke," he said fiercely. "Any unwanted penetration. Doesn't require a penis. Your therapist should have told you that."

Silence hung between them for a long, long moment. "I didn't tell her. I didn't tell anyone."

The significance of her admission wasn't lost on him. A hard knot formed in his throat. "Damn, angel," he said tightly. "You've been carrying this burden for too long. But I'm glad you told me."

"Don't tell Grace. Please don't."

"I'm not telling anyone, baby. I wouldn't. I think you should tell your therapist though. It's important to helping you heal."

She sighed, her fingers curling into his shirt. "I know it sounds impossible, but I already feel better for having told you."

"That's good. Really good. But it's probably not

enough, okay? You should still tell your therapist so she can help you process it."

"I will. Thank you, Cade."

He dragged in a breath and pressed his lips to her hair. She'd kept silent for so long. Too long. She'd been carrying this weight alone when she should've had support. And now she thanked him like he'd taken out the trash for her instead of listening to her spill something so personal and traumatic.

"You ready to look at me now or do you need to stand here for a while?" he asked.

Because he knew that she liked to hide behind barriers when she felt vulnerable. First the texting and now this with her cheek pressed to his chest as she spilled her darkest secrets to him. Not that he minded holding her.

"Can we just stand here for few minutes?"

"Whatever you need."

"You're amazing, Cade Rodgers with a *D*."

"So are you, Brooke Sullivan with an *E*."

They stood there for a long while, holding each other while Cade systematically planned and executed a murder in his mind. He wouldn't do it, but it sure felt damned good to think about it. Hurting Brooke was like hurting a kitten. Anybody who did that didn't deserve to live.

And anybody who tried from this moment forward was going to have to go through him to do it.

Chapter 12

Brooke stared out the window on the way back to her condo. She couldn't think of anything to say now that she'd basically told Cade the worst thing that had ever happened to her. In the scheme of things, it could have been much worse. She hadn't endured something so terrible she couldn't get over it. So many people endured so much worse than that.

She'd been groped. Violated. Threatened with violence. She'd gone from a world in which everything made sense to her, in which her choices were *her* choices and no one could force their will upon her, to a world in which she was no longer safe. She'd learned in the space of a heartbeat that she wasn't really in charge of what happened to her, and it had terrified her.

She didn't trust people. Didn't trust their motives. It had taken her almost two years to work up to dating a man, to being alone with him. Scott hadn't been threatening, but she'd still had to force herself to see him the first time. When there'd been no spark, she'd blamed herself and gone on another date.

But she'd quickly realized she wasn't ever going to get to a place where there were sparks with him.

There were sparks with Cade. Lots of sparks. Cannons of sparks. He didn't scare her on a physical level, though his life as a warrior scared her. How did Grace stand it? How did she watch Garrett go off on a mission and not lose her mind?

Brooke asked herself if it was worth the risk getting involved with him would mean. But she was already involved. She'd told him her darkest secret, the thing that had kept her up at night for so long. The thing that had made her feel broken. It wasn't just the violent way she'd been ripped from her bed and threatened. It was the way she'd had no control over who had touched her body and how.

Cade said it was rape. There was a certain comfort in having someone believe her and in being free to call it by so violent a name. She'd been raped. Not in the conventional way, not for long, but a man had shoved his fingers into her body and told her he was going to do whatever he wanted to her.

That he'd never gotten the chance didn't change the fact he'd violated her body. Or the feelings she'd carried for so long. Why hadn't she told Dr. Higgs what had happened? Dr. Higgs would have understood. It was her job to understand.

But Brooke had always been intimidated by the doctor. From the moment Dr. Higgs had seen her shortly after she'd been rescued, Brooke had thought that the doctor was a woman who couldn't possibly be anything but in control of her circumstances. She was just too confident and self-aware.

Brooke sighed and rubbed her temple. That was a crock of shit and she knew it. Anyone could be ripped from what they knew and thrust into a nightmare. *Anyone.*

"You okay?"

She gritted her teeth and then turned to Cade with as sunny a smile as she could muster. "Of course."

He flexed his fingers on the wheel, and she knew he didn't believe her. Cade knew her pretty well for someone who'd only been in her life a short time.

"Not really," she admitted. "I've fought myself for so long, rejecting the term *rape* because it seemed too strong. Like it made me a crybaby when other women have gone through worse. I'm mad at myself for it and mad I didn't tell Dr. Higgs. Maybe I could have avoided wallowing in self-pity for so long if I had."

"Angel, self-pity is allowed when you've gone through something traumatic. Nobody gets to tell you how to feel."

She stared at him in amazement. "Why do you make me feel so normal?"

He glanced at her. "Because you are. If you were locked up in your house, refusing to leave, not eating or showering or taking your dog out for a walk—well, then I'd say you weren't normal. But you are. This is life, angel. It's what we do."

They turned into the parking garage of her building and drove to her guest spot. Cade grabbed his backpack and waited for her to precede him into the building. She swiped her key card at the entry and the door opened.

"Do you need a card for entry everywhere?" he asked from behind her.

"This is the only other entry, besides the lobby, but that's staffed twenty-four hours a day. You need a card to get into the building from the garage."

"But you can walk into the front entry without one."

"Yes, but visitors are supposed to check in."

"Supposed to. Presumably they don't have to."

"No, I guess they don't. But if a guard didn't recognize someone, he would ask for identification."

Cade looked thoughtful. "What about service entrances? What are the procedures there?"

Brooke frowned. She hadn't considered that. What if Scott's killer hadn't passed the front desk after all? Could he have just entered the building through one of the delivery entrances? "I don't know. Do you think that's how the man came in?"

"It's possible. Or it's possible he didn't use his real name when he checked in."

"You mean he had a false name and Scott either knew it was fake or only knew him by that name?"

"Either one. But the service entrance seems the more likely route if he didn't want to be seen."

They reached the elevator and stepped in. Max sat quietly as Cade punched the button for her floor.

"But wouldn't there be some sort of security procedure for the service entrance?"

"Should be. But maybe he paid somebody off."

"You make it all sound like cloak-and-dagger stuff."

His eyes were troubled. "It's my job to think that way. But angel, you don't really think it was a random event, do you? Scott Lloyd was involved in something or knew something he shouldn't. It's the most logical explanation."

Brooke put her hand on Max's head for comfort. "I know. But that doesn't mean I like it. What if I'd been with him? What if that man had shown up the night Scott wanted me to have dinner with him?"

"But he didn't. Don't dwell on the what-ifs."

She knew he was right, though the thought lived in the back of her mind. Part of the reason she didn't want to be alone just yet. But Cade had a life, and he wasn't staying forever. She would have to get her shit together soon if she was going to face the nights alone.

"I know you're right. I just get a little paranoid, I guess."

"Understandable. But don't let it eat you up inside. Besides, I'm here. Nobody's getting through me, Brooke."

The steel in his words made her shiver. "You'll have to go home soon. Back to your life."

"I'm right where I need to be. Where I want to be. And I'm staying as long as you need me."

She shook her head. "Don't say that to me, Cade. I'll ask you to stay for much longer than I should. Just because I hate being alone."

THEY ORDERED TAKEOUT, then settled in to watch a

movie together. They sat on Brooke's couch while Max lay on the floor nearby. When Cade lifted his arm and put it on the back of the couch, he gave Brooke a significant look. It was up to her whether or not to sit next to him. When she scooted into the circle of his embrace, he was both pleased and stunned.

She'd been through a lot, more than she'd told anyone else, and he was well aware how traumatic it had been for her. He was still pissed that some asshole motherfucker had violated her body. He'd been thinking hard about how he was going to approach the two of them getting physical, and he finally decided that the way to do it was to make his intentions known and then let her make the final decision.

She snuggled against his side as a romantic comedy began to play. Not his typical type of thing, but he'd let her choose it. He regretted it the instant the sexy scenes started. They weren't porn or anything, but they featured a naked actress with bouncing boobs pretending to fuck a guy silly.

He wouldn't mind being fucked silly right about now. Except this was Brooke, and she wasn't likely to consider such a proposition just yet. Hell, maybe not ever. Which was a depressing thought if he let himself dwell on it.

"Sorry," she said after the second scene of people pretending to fuck. "Maybe this was a bad idea."

"It's giving me ideas, but I can handle it," he told her gruffly.

She pushed herself upright and looked at him. "I'm not sure I can."

Jesus, he wanted to kiss her. But he wouldn't. *Let her make the first move.* "Then let's find something else."

"How about *Doctor Who*? That's pretty unsexy."

"Never seen it," he admitted.

Her eyes widened. "Never seen *Doctor Who*? Seriously? Oh my God, Cade! You have no idea what you're missing!"

She was so excited that he began to get curious. He'd heard of *Doctor Who*. Of course he had. He'd just never watched it.

"We have to start with season one of the reboot, which is the ninth doctor—" She waved a hand before he could ask what the hell she meant. "Never mind, don't worry about it. You'll catch on soon enough. But it's cheesy at first, okay? Production values get much better as the series goes on. It's like the BBC sent up a test balloon, the cheapest one they could find, and when it did well, they suddenly threw a massive budget behind it. Anyway, *Doctor Who* is amazing. You'll love it, I promise."

He didn't know if he would, but he wasn't going to tell her that. "Then I guess I have to see it."

She grabbed the remote and started scrolling through her programs. "You really do. But if you don't love it, just tell me, okay? We can find something else."

He loved that she cared whether or not he liked her show. And there was no fucking way, even if he hated the damned thing, he'd ever tell her differently. Not when it made her sparkle with happiness like this.

"I'm all in, babe. Let's do this."

Somewhere around the fifth episode, she fell asleep.

He could tell because of the way her body went limp against his. She'd been right though—the show was interesting as hell. The Doctor had his hands full with Rose and all the adventures they went on. Cade finished the episode, then turned everything off and gently picked up Brooke. She put her arms around his neck and curled herself into him as he carried her to bed. He wanted nothing more than to climb in there with her, but that wasn't the best idea because he'd want to do more than lie next to her. So he put her down and pulled up the covers.

She mumbled something but didn't wake. He left her there and went out to clip on Max's leash and take him out one more time. Bert was at the desk and they chatted a bit. Cade asked about procedures for the service entrance. Bert was happy to fill him in. There was a list of the contractors who were allowed daily access. They didn't have key cards, but they had identification credentials that allowed them inside once they were checked against the list. Which meant that the man who'd killed Scott Lloyd had either had connections that'd gotten him on the list or he'd bribed someone.

Max did his business and Cade took him upstairs, waving Brooke's key card over the door to get inside. His phone rang a few seconds later. It was Hacker.

"Been doing some digging," Hacker said. "You aren't going to believe this shit."

Cade's gut tightened. "What?"

"Black Eagle Firearms is being investigated for possible weapons sales to drug cartels in South America. Entire caches of weapons missing from the shipping manifests—and Scott Lloyd just returned from South America a couple of days ago."

"Shit."

"Yeah. The ATF and DEA were working this one together. Ivy McGill Erikson is lead on the DEA side."

Ivy was married to Dane "Viking" Erikson, the leader of the first SEAL team to join HOT. Which meant cooperation was presumably easier to come by than if they went in cold. That was a plus at least.

"Any idea who bought the weapons? Or where they are?"

"Andreas Lopez is the man Lloyd met in Bogota. He's with the Espinoza Cartel. But so far as we know, the cartel hasn't received any new weapon shipments lately."

"Any ID on the man in the security footage from Brooke's building?"

Hacker hesitated a moment. "That's the funny part, Saint. There is no man in the footage. It's been erased in two spots, presumably his entrance and exit. There's nothing to tie him to Lloyd's murder."

"Nothing except Brooke Sullivan."

"Pretty much."

Cade didn't like the way his stomach twisted at the news. "So how was it done? Somebody hack in? Or an inside job?"

Hacker sighed. "That I don't know yet. But I do know this. You better watch out for Brooke. Right now she's the only person who can ID the man who shot Scott Lloyd."

Chapter 13

Brooke watched as Cade unhooked his jeans and slid them down his thighs. His cock sprang free, hard and big, and she moaned at the sight of it. Her heart raced and sweat prickled her skin, but she was far more interested than she was frightened. This was Cade, and he wouldn't hurt her.

"Yes," she said as he moved toward her. "Please, yes."

He sank down on top of her, and she opened her arms and legs, welcoming him. She wanted the press of him inside her body, the sensation of fullness that would come with it. She hadn't had sex in so long and she missed it. There was a moment of panic, and then it was gone.

Because she trusted him. Because Cade wouldn't hurt her.

He lay on top of her, not inside her yet, but she could feel the tip of him at her entrance.

"Brooke," he said. "Brooke."

"Oh yes, baby. *Yes*," she urged.

"Brooke. Wake up."

Wake up? What?

Brooke's eyes snapped open. Cade hovered over her, but he wasn't lying on top of her. He also wasn't naked.

Heat flooded her. And confusion. "Cade?"

"Yes, angel. You need to get up."

She wasn't quite processing what he was saying. The dream was fading but not easily. "Up? Why?"

"Trust me, angel. I need you awake, okay? We're leaving."

That got her attention. Ice rolled down her spine and into her toes. "Leaving? Why?"

"I'll tell you on the way. But we need to get out of here."

Brooke sat up and rubbed her eyes. Just a short while ago, they'd been eating takeout and watching television. What the hell?

"You're scaring me, Cade."

He looked apologetic as he loomed over her, holding her jacket in his hands. "I'm sorry about that. But we've got to go."

Fear perched on her shoulder like an icy cloud. She shoved the covers back and sat on the side of the bed. She was still in her yoga pants and T-shirt, so at least she was mostly covered. Her shoes were beside the bed and she slipped them on, tying them as she looked up at him.

"I need to get some clothes."

"No time. I put some stuff in a bag. Max is ready. I packed food and his bowl."

"What's going on, Cade?"

"I'll tell you when we're clear. Right now we need to go."

Brooke got to her feet, but her legs wouldn't obey the command to move.

"Now, angel."

"I-I can't move, Cade. I'm scared." She hated saying it. Hated sounding so damned pitiful, but all she could do was remember that night when she'd been dragged from her bed and forced into a van. The nightmare had only been beginning then.

Cade came to her side and put an arm around her shoulders. "I've got you, angel. I've got you, and nobody's going to hurt you. But I won't lie to you. It turns out that Scott Lloyd was associated with some bad shit. I think it's best if we get away from here while his killer is still on the loose."

"But I don't know anything about what Scott was doing. I'm not involved in any way."

"I know. But it'll be safer if we go. We don't know who'll come looking for information about Scott, so it's best if you aren't here."

"Okay," she said, her body shaking with fear. She told herself this was nothing like the night she'd been ripped from her bed, but the urgency in Cade's tone didn't help. Still, she sucked down the terror and went with Cade to the living room. He had a couple of bags sitting by the door.

"Is there anything else you need?" he asked.

"My computer?"

"Got it."

She didn't know that she'd be able to work but maybe. "Meds?"

"Yep."

"I can't think, Cade. You're scaring me."

He took her in his arms, holding her close for a quick moment. "I'm sorry. I really am. If I need to come back for something, I will. But my instincts tell me we need to go, and I never ignore my instincts."

"I trust you."

He gave her a squeeze and then let her go. "I know, angel."

They gathered the bags, got Max, and left the building as quickly and quietly as possible. They took the elevator to the garage instead of the lobby. Cade tossed everything in his truck, put Max in the back seat and clipped him into the doggie seat belt she'd left in his truck earlier, and helped her inside. She shivered as she scanned the garage, her paranoia putting her on high alert.

Cade jumped into the other side and started the vehicle. Soon they were slipping through the garage and down toward the exit. Brooke couldn't find her voice as she darted her gaze around, looking for evil men lurking behind corners. When they emerged from the garage and turned onto the street, she breathed a sigh of relief.

"What time is it?" she asked, realizing she hadn't checked the time before now. And oh hell, where was her phone?

"It's a little after one. Your phone is in your purse along with your charger."

She blinked at him. How did he know what she was thinking?

"The last thing I remember is Rose and the Doctor battling the aliens."

"You fell asleep. I carried you to bed."

That explained the yoga pants and the fact she was still wearing her bra. She shook herself, trying to clear her brain. "How did we get from you carrying me to bed to running away in the middle of the night?"

He glanced at her. "Information from my team. Scott was involved in weapons black marketing to drug cartels in South America. Seemed prudent to leave."

Brooke tried to process the anger that flared deep inside. Scott had been selling guns? All the while he'd been trying to get her into a relationship with him, he'd been doing something illegal. Even when he'd known she'd been abducted because of her relationship to Grace, he'd still thought nothing of pulling her into his life.

She thought of him returning her books, acting so hurt that she'd told him she didn't want to get involved, and anger scoured through her like a flame. *The bastard!*

"How does any of this affect me? I only went out with Scott a few times, and we weren't involved at all. I don't know anything about his business."

Cade's fingers flexed on the wheel, and she knew it was bad news. "The man you saw outside the elevator… he isn't on the security feed at all."

Brooke's stomach dropped. "How is that possible?"

"I don't know. But it's not good." He glanced into

the rearview and frowned. "I think we might have a tail."

BEHIND THEM, a car's headlights shone bright. Not that it was unusual in a city this size, but whenever he turned, the car did too. Not only that, but it kept a reasonable distance, never slowing or speeding up. Cade was suspicious of shit like that, so he decided it was time to do a test.

"Hang on, angel," he said, whipping the wheel hard left and onto a side street.

Brooke squeaked. Cade mashed the gas and the truck leaped into action like a raptor taking flight.

The headlights appeared behind him, speeding toward them down the street. Someone had been watching Brooke's building. Not only that, but they knew he was there with her. So if they were chasing him now, they'd probably been close enough to see that Brooke was with him.

Son of a bitch, he should have made her lie down on the seat. He hadn't considered it because he'd thought he was ahead of the curve. He should have fucking known better.

Then again, whoever'd killed Scott Lloyd had been able to erase security footage. If they could do that, they could also watch and see when Brooke left the building.

Shit.

Cade stomped on the gas and hit the button on his

steering wheel to activate hands-free mode. "Call Hacker," he said, and the phone began to dial.

"Yeah, man." Hacker's voice was crisp and businesslike.

"Got a tail. Left Brooke's building and someone was waiting for us."

"Where are you?"

Cade checked the GPS and rattled off the street and cross streets as they passed each one.

"Hang on," Hacker said, and Cade could hear the clicking of keys on the keyboard. "Okay, see that red light up ahead?"

"Yeah," Cade replied. It was in the distance but getting closer quickly.

"Take a hard right there. Then another hard right. There's a small alley. Drive down it until you come to a cross alley and then make a left. Turn off the lights and wait."

Cade didn't even question his teammate because Hacker knew his stuff. Brooke could hear the whole conversation, but she wasn't saying anything. He thought she might be praying.

Cade barreled toward the intersection, then swung hard right at the last moment. He floored the pedal, then jammed the brake and swung hard right again. The cross alley loomed and he pulled a left, stomped the brake and engaged the emergency brake, then flicked off the lights.

Max panted in the back seat. Brooke didn't utter a sound, but her chin dropped and she closed her eyes.

"Anything?" Hacker asked.

"Nothing yet." The buildings were close together, and the alleys were literally small access roads that ran behind them. It was a good place to hide because you'd have to drive right up on someone's ass to find them.

"Wait ten minutes. If he doesn't show up, I'll talk you out. There's a network of small alleys you can traverse until you get to the highway. Which direction you want to go?"

"Get me back to Maryland. After that, I'm probably gonna head south. Get a hotel room somewhere quiet for the night."

"Copy that."

"Got to mute you for a minute," Cade said as he glanced at Brooke.

Her face was white and she had a hand over her heart.

"Go ahead."

Cade pressed the Mute button and touched Brooke's shoulder. "You okay, angel?"

She glanced up at him, blinking rapidly. "I'm okay. Just feel a little panicky. I never expected…" She shook her head. "Yeah, I never thought I'd be in this kind of situation again. It's a little overwhelming."

"A little?" He said it teasingly, and she smiled for a second before frowning again.

"Okay, a lot overwhelming. But I'm better prepared now. I have you, I have Max, and I took a self-defense class."

"Sounds like you've got it covered then." He grinned and she smiled back.

"Yes, I think I do."

"Don't worry, Brooke. I know what I'm doing."

"And if they find us before the ten minutes are up?"

"Nobody's getting to you without going through me. And believe me, that isn't happening. Not my first rodeo."

Her smile was shaky. "I said I hated guns, but right now I'm pretty happy you have one."

He winked. "I have two on me. Both hold fifteen rounds per magazine. Plus I've got extra mags. We're good."

She turned to look at Max, who sat watching them both, tongue lolling out as he panted. "You okay, Maxie?"

His tail thumped the seat, and Brooke reached back to scratch him. Cade checked his watch and then scanned the mirrors and the street. Nothing happened. He unmuted the phone and told Hacker he was back.

"Five more minutes," Hacker said.

"Can you check for some motels on the route?"

"I can do better than that. I can book you something under an assumed name."

"Yeah, sounds good."

"I'll send details to your phone." He tapped some keys. "What's the plan tomorrow?"

"I think we'd better plan for a meeting with Ghost." Ghost was Alex Bishop, HOT's second-in-command. He was a hell of an operator, and he'd more than proven himself to the guys when he'd taken over the unsanctioned shadow-ops mission to rescue Mendez in Russia.

Ghost was the guy you went to first. Mendez, or

Viper as he was also known, was the big kahuna, the man in charge, and these days his plate was so full he didn't need to be bothered until necessary.

"Copy that. Okay, got you a reservation, Mr. Jones. Sending over the details. And we've got two minutes to go."

Brooke sat quietly, hands folded in her lap. Cade wanted to kiss her for luck, but he didn't. The two minutes passed and nothing happened—no cars careening down the lane, no gunfire, no yelling or screaming.

"Ready to go?" Hacker asked.

Cade put his foot on the brake and released the emergency brake. Then he flipped on the lights. "Ready. Now get us the fuck out of here, buddy."

"Copy that, Saint."

Chapter 14

Brooke felt like she hardly breathed for the entire trip through DC and into Maryland. She kept glancing at Cade, knowing that if someone was tailing them again, he would know. But nothing happened and no cars seemed to be following them.

It took over an hour to reach the motel Hacker had booked for them. It was a small strip motel on the outskirts of some small town along the route. Brooke eyed it dubiously as they turned into the parking lot. Cade drove around the rear and backed into a slot.

They got their things and Max and went to check in. The night manager eyed the dog, groused about a pet deposit, which Cade paid in cash, and then handed them the key.

"Room 136. Upstairs, last room at the end."

"Thanks."

They left the motel office and headed for the stairs that would lead them up.

"You stand here and I'll take Max into the grass," Cade told her when they reached the bottom of the steps.

She would have protested, but she was too tired. "Okay. Thanks."

Max sniffed around a bit but did his business when Cade firmly told him to pee. Then they returned, and Cade lifted his gear while handing her Max's leash.

She went upstairs first and Cade followed. He inserted the key in the lock and swung the door open while Brooke braced herself for a disaster.

But the room was clean, if dated, and it smelled like lemon oil and pine. Those were the scents of her childhood, the way she'd known that Mom had been cleaning all day and everything was fresh. Add lavender to the linens and the picture would be complete.

Cade stowed their bags against the wall. There was a dresser, a queen-size bed, a bathroom, and a small couch against one wall. Max immediately bounded up on the couch while Brooke told him to get down. He looked at her with such a sad face she frowned.

"Let him be," Cade said. "Neither one of us will fit on it anyway."

She swallowed as she realized the implications of that declaration.

"Relax, angel," he told her, and she knew her face must have shown her thoughts. "We can sleep in the same bed without touching."

Her skin flamed. "How do you always know what I'm thinking?"

"Because I know you," he said simply, and her heart

137

squeezed. If she hadn't called him to pick her up from the hospital, he wouldn't be here right now. Then again, she might not be here either. And that could be a whole lot worse for her.

"I've gotten you into a mess you didn't bargain for, but I'm so glad I called you to come get me, Cade."

"I live my life getting into messes—and getting back out again. It's fine."

Brooke rubbed her arms. If she'd called Grace, her friend's Secret Service protection would have extended to her while they were together. But it wouldn't have lasted, and Brooke was fairly certain Grace's guards wouldn't share information with her the way Cade did.

"How long do we have to do this?" she asked.

"I really don't know, angel. I'm sorry."

Brooke sank onto the end of the bed and rubbed her hands through her hair. Emotion simmered beneath the surface, swirling and boiling and trying to break free. But whether she'd scream or cry or yell, she didn't know.

Her life had been normal—or as normal as it ever was for her—just a couple of days ago. She'd been doing her work, taking care of her dog, and sexting with a handsome hunk of a military man. She might have gone on that way forever—well, except for the sexting because he definitely would have stopped doing that before too long—if she hadn't taken Max out for a walk at precisely the time she did.

Strike that. It wasn't the going for a walk so much as the choice of when to return. *That* was the mistake.

"Maybe if I go to sleep, I'll wake up and find out the whole thing was a nightmare."

She remembered, forcefully, the dream she'd been having when he'd woken her just a couple of hours ago. He'd been about to slide into her body when the dream evaporated and she was being shaken awake instead.

Heat blossomed between her thighs. She didn't really know what Cade looked like naked, but she'd seen most of him in the pictures he sent her. She'd seen the bulge, but not the real thing. Suddenly she wanted to see him. She wanted to know what it felt like to have him inside her, to feel his penis slide between her folds and fill her. Would it be amazing? Or would she chicken out and beg him to stop?

He lifted his shirt and extracted a weapon that he laid on the table beside the bed. Another gun appeared and he laid that on the table too. Brooke pulled in a shaky breath.

He peeled his shirt off his body with one hand, then turned to face her. She snapped her jaw closed and tried not to focus on the acres of muscle adorned with ink in a few places. But oh, he was so lovely. So perfect.

The old Brooke would have wanted to run her tongue over those peaks and valleys, sliding her way down his washboard abdomen to the root of him. And then she'd have wanted to slide his cock into her mouth and lick it too.

The new Brooke was jumping up and down inside and yelling, *Me too! Me too! Let's do it!*

But that was too big a leap. Maybe a smaller leap was needed. Something she could handle. Something that wasn't threatening.

"You want the bathroom first?" he asked.

Brooke shook her head.

"You okay, angel? The guns are loaded, but they won't hurt you lying there. I need them close by, or I'd make sure you didn't see them."

"It's okay," she croaked out. "It's fine."

He frowned. "Something wrong?"

"No. Yes." She closed her eyes and blurted it out because she'd never be able to say it otherwise. "I want you to kiss me."

CADE FROZE. Kiss her? Holy hell, he wanted that pretty damned badly. He wanted a lot more than that too. He wanted his tongue in her mouth, and then he wanted his tongue in her pussy, licking her into a shuddering orgasm that had her screaming his name.

He'd dreamed about it. Pressing her back on the bed, sliding her ridiculously tiny panties from her hips, spreading her legs open and sinking between them where he'd taste her while she shivered and shook and moaned.

But fucking hell, she'd asked for a kiss. It was monumental for her, and he knew that. *Let her come to you.*

That had been his strategy, and it had worked. But it was also a big responsibility. He couldn't scare her with his raging desire for her.

"Honey, I want that more than you know. But you're going to have to tell me how you want it. Do I treat you like glass and give you a chaste peck on the lips, or do I hold you close and slip you some tongue? And if I slip you some tongue, I'm going to get hard. Not that I'll expect to do anything with it, but it'll be there between us, and I'd rather not have to contort myself to hide it from you."

Hell, he was already hard. But she didn't need to know it.

Her gaze dropped to the floor. She was so cute in her yoga pants and jacket, her tennis shoes so small on her feet. Her hair was a messy tangle of golden strands, and her chest rose and fell a little more rapidly than it had a few seconds ago.

"I want the real kiss, Cade. I trust you. And I know, no matter how aroused you might be, you'd never force me to do anything I didn't want to do."

His throat was tight. "You're right, I wouldn't. But how do you know that for sure?"

She shrugged, her expression suddenly shy. "I just do. If I can't trust you— Well, how will I ever trust anyone?"

"I'm not sure I deserve that kind of trust, angel. I'm just a man trying his best to be a good guy instead of a dick."

Her blue eyes snapped to his. "You couldn't be a dick if you tried. You're too decent. You've been nothing but decent to me."

It was work to contain the inner beast that wanted out. The one that wanted to conquer and pleasure this woman until she couldn't stand. Until she couldn't think a single thought except his name.

"Just so you know, Brooke... You're my favorite dirty thought. The first dirty thought of my day and the last in the evening. I imagine you naked, beneath me, surrounding me. What I'm thinking is anything but decent."

"Are you trying to scare me on purpose?"

He shrugged. "Maybe. I don't know. I just know that I'm not pure when it comes to you—and you need to know it."

"I think your texts were clear on that," she said with a hint of humor. "You told me what you wanted to do to me. But I want to start with a kiss. Just a kiss."

She was going to be the death of him.

"Okay." He closed the distance between them and dragged her softly into his arms. She sucked in a breath and gripped his biceps before her fingers relaxed and went to his pecs. She smiled up at him so trustingly that his heart ached.

Holy fuck, she was beautiful. Would she taste as sweet as she looked?

"If it gets to be too much, tell me stop, angel. Don't hesitate, don't try to think your way through it, don't keep going for fear of making me angry. Tell me to stop, and I will."

Her eyes were so innocent. "It's just a kiss, Cade. How can it be too much?"

He chuckled deep in his throat. "Oh baby, you have no idea. You ready?"

She nodded. He skimmed his palm along her jaw and into her hair, massaging the back of her head as he tipped her back with a gentle tug on the long strands. Not much, because it would scare her, but enough to let her know what he wanted.

She was small in his arms, a pixie to his giant. He could pick her up and not even feel like he was having to do much work. But he wouldn't do that yet. Later.

He pulled her in closer, close enough to feel his erection, and dropped his mouth to hers by slow degrees. She closed her eyes at the last second and he stopped, gazing down at her, at her pink mouth, parted slightly, her lashes fanning her cheeks, her creamy skin flushed and slightly rosy.

She wanted the kiss. There was no doubt about that. He cupped her skull with one hand and slid the other down to her buttocks, pressing her hips tighter to his body.

And then he kissed her, a gentle claiming of her mouth with his own. She moaned softly, her mouth dropping open a little wider than before. He hesitated to enter, but she had no such fears. Her tongue darted out to meet his, tangling with him in a sensual duel.

Cade's knees went weak. Literally weak. He didn't buckle, but he damn sure wondered what the hell it was about. Still, he kept kissing her, plundering her mouth, driving deeper with each thrust. She didn't stiffen or cry out or push him away.

She clung to him, her mouth as ravenous as his, her tongue searching and seeking as her arms went around his neck and tightened. If she were any other woman, he'd have her tits in his hands right now. But he couldn't do that. Not with her, and not without express permission.

There was no room for the typical give and take of seduction. He needed to know what she wanted, and he needed to take it absolutely no farther than what she allowed.

And yet two weeks' worth of fantasies and naughty texts were working in his head, making him think about all the ways in which he wanted to explore this woman. Anybody else and he'd be ripping her shirt off and filling his hands and mouth with her luscious breasts.

Then he'd lick his way down her abdomen, rip off her yoga pants, and sink his face into her center.

He did none of that, of course. He simply held Brooke tightly to him and devoured her mouth, licking, kissing, nipping. Her moans told him she approved. Her arms around his neck told him she wasn't afraid. The arching of her body against his told him she was aroused.

They kissed for a long time, sucking and devouring and moaning until Cade's balls ached from the lack of a pressure release valve, until he had to stop kissing her and set her away before he took the next step.

She gazed up at him, blinking, while he held her at arm's length.

"I can't keep doing this, angel," he said roughly. "I want you too much."

She licked her lips, her tongue swiping a wet trail over the bottom one, and he wanted to suck it into his mouth and make her moan.

"I want more too."

Jesus.

"Angel, you told me you haven't had sex in two years —maybe you need to slow it down a bit before we take this too far and you regret it."

She shook her blond head, hair shimmering in the dim light of the lamps. "Maybe I've been taking it slow for too long. Maybe I need to plunge full speed ahead and see where this takes me."

He wanted to pounce—yet he hesitated. "You know the kinds of things I want to do to you, Brooke. I've told you many nights, haven't I? While you stroked your pussy and begged me for more. But this is *real*, baby. As real as it gets. You're asking for me to do all those things to you for real. And once we've gone there, once we've tasted each other—there's no going back. We burn through this thing together until the end. You need to be sure, and I'm not at all certain one kiss—no matter how hot—is enough to make that decision."

She frowned. "We've had more than a kiss. We've shared a lot over the past couple of weeks. I'm certain I don't want that to end anytime soon. Sex is a logical step, right?"

His heart hammered. "It is a logical step. But until two days ago, you refused to even talk to me on the phone. Now you want to leap past dating and talking to sex?"

Her gaze didn't waver. "Yes, Cade. That is exactly what I want."

Chapter 15

Oh my God, she was seriously insane. But she'd had a lot of time to think on the ride, and she'd decided that she'd been stupid to keep Cade to texting. Stupid that she'd never moved past their text conversations to phone calls or, yes, dating.

Still, this was a *huge* leap. Her heart fluttered like a trapped butterfly, and her skin sizzled to a million degrees as his hot gaze pierced through her. He was so big, so overwhelming, but he touched her tenderly. He didn't shove his tongue down her throat or do anything she didn't want him to do.

Hell, he hadn't done anything at all except kiss the living daylights out of her. Make her crazy with need. She'd wanted to climb up his body and wrap her arms and legs around him and never let go. She'd thought a small leap was needed, a kiss only, and then maybe she could think about doing something more at another time.

She'd been wrong.

Right now she was wet, aroused, and dying for some relief. Was she scared? Partly yes. But mostly no. Cade was *nothing* like the man who'd forced his way into her body with his fingers. If she told Cade to stop, he would stop.

Brooke believed it with every fiber of her being. He was a risk she was willing to take.

He didn't move, and she knew he was considering how to tell her no, it wasn't time, they needed to wait.

But she didn't want to wait anymore. She was done with waiting. Someone had chased them tonight, someone who presumably wanted to hurt her. What if they'd succeeded? She wouldn't have known what it was like to be with this man, to explore his body and let him explore hers.

And she desperately wanted those things. She was tired of hiding, of cowering alone in her apartment. She'd told Grace that it was time she started living and she meant that. She hadn't known how much she'd meant it until Cade had kissed her.

She glanced at the couch where Max lay, head on his paws, watching the two of them. That wasn't going to work. She strode into the bathroom and called him. He came trotting in. Thankfully it wasn't tiny. She patted his head, told him to stay, and shut the door. He'd be okay for a while, just until she did what she needed to do.

Cade hadn't moved from where he'd been standing. Though it scared her a little, Brooke shrugged out of her jacket, grasped the hem of her T-shirt and yanked it up and over her head.

"Angel," Cade growled.

"It gets better, Cade," she said, reaching behind her back to unsnap her bra. She hesitated for a moment before sliding the straps down her arms and tossing the garment on the bed.

Cool air caressed her nipples, making them tighten and stand up straight. Cade choked out a word, but she didn't hear it past the rushing of blood in her ears.

She toed off her shoes and hooked her thumbs into her yoga pants. A moment later, she dragged them off and dropped them. That left only her panties, a tiny G-string number with lace and sparkly threads.

"Brooke, holy hell," Cade said.

She couldn't bring herself to remove the panties, as if that single scrap of fabric could protect her if he refused her offering.

"I want you, Cade. Not an eggplant or a tongue emoji. You, doing all those things you promised me. Do you even know how, or do you spend your nights making that stuff up to help lonely women get off?"

She had to tease him or she'd lose her nerve. He didn't say anything for a long moment, and she began to worry. But then he swore. A moment later, he dragged her against him, naked flesh to naked flesh, and she moaned with the sheer excitement of it. He was big and hard, but he was also gentle with her.

"Here's what's going to happen," he growled. "I'm going to kiss every inch of you, Brooke Sullivan. I'm going to kiss and caress your naked skin until you can't stand to be touched another moment, and then I'm going to lick your sweet pussy until you're as limp as a wet noodle. If, at that point, you still want more, I'm gonna fill you with my cock and take you over the edge one more time. At any time if you want to stop, you tell me to stop. That will be the end of it. Understand?"

All she could do was nod. He put an arm around her waist and one under her ass and lifted her. Brooke instinctively put her legs around him. He held her high against him so that she was looking down at him. His gray eyes were so serious as he gazed up at her.

"You're pretty special, angel," he told her. "You do things to me... Hell, I don't know what it is or why, but I know I don't want to do anything to jeopardize that. I need to be in your life, Brooke."

If her heart hadn't already melted before, it certainly would have with those words. He made her want to cry. And he scared her too, because when had the good things lasted for her? Her entire life had been turned upside down two years ago—what if it happened again? What if he couldn't handle her craziness once he got what he wanted?

"I need you too, Cade. So much." It was the truth. Not just physically but in her life. She *needed* Cade Rodgers. It hit her suddenly what that really meant. She'd watched Grace and Garrett for so long, and she'd envied them. Her friend was head over heels in love with her husband.

And Brooke was head over heels in love with Cade. It ought to be impossible, but it wasn't. She loved him and needed him in her life.

A spark of fear flared deep inside. He'd said she did things to him, but he'd also said he didn't know what it was. He needed her in his life—but that wasn't love. He hadn't said he loved her.

Crushing fear threatened her happiness, but she squeezed her eyes shut and forced it away. Nothing was going to ruin this moment with Cade. Nothing was going to mar her happiness at what she was about to do.

"We shouldn't be doing this here," he said. "You deserve better. Not a cheap motel in a small town but a soft bed with satin sheets and rose petals or something romantic like that."

"Just being with you is romantic, Cade. We've had two weeks of foreplay. I don't need anything more than you."

"Put your hand over my heart."

She did as he told her. His heart pounded beneath her palm.

"You do that to me," he said. "I want you to know that before we go any further. This isn't just a hookup, and I need you to believe that."

"I do believe it."

His gray eyes searched hers. "Remember to stop me if you don't like something. Even if you change your mind entirely. Tell me to stop."

She put her fingers over his mouth. "Enough, Cade. I know the drill. And I trust you. There's nothing more to say."

He lowered her slowly until their faces were close. She didn't wait for him to make the first move. She closed the distance between them and kissed him, her tongue sliding into his mouth and finding his. It was sheer heaven to kiss Cade Rodgers.

He took his time, his mouth moving against hers, his hard body holding hers. His arm beneath her ass supported her, and his other hand was free to roam around to her front. He skimmed his fingers beneath her breast and goose bumps rose on her skin. Then he pinched her nipple between his thumb and forefinger and a lightning bolt of heat and need sizzled straight down into her core.

"Is that okay?" he asked, and she loved that he did so. He was thinking of what she'd told him about her captor, but the way he touched her was nothing like what that man had done. It wasn't vile and it didn't make her skin crawl.

No, it made her skin glow and her nerve endings dance.

"Yes," she said—moaned, really. "That's perfect, Cade."

"Pretty angel," he said, putting his lips against her neck, lifting her with that broad arm supporting her, trailing his mouth down her neck and toward the sloping flesh of her cleavage.

Brooke had never wanted anything as much as she wanted Cade to lick her nipple right that moment. He seemed to know it too, because he licked a trail around it without actually touching it. Her fingers curled into his shoulders.

"Cade. Please."

His chuckle was a hum against her skin. "Please what, Brooke?"

"You know what."

His tongue darted out and swiped across her nipple. "Yeah, I know."

She moaned. "You're evil."

"Nope. Just making you squirm a little. Makes it that much better when it happens."

"I'm ready for it to happen, Cade. Now."

He laughed and then fastened his mouth over her nipple and sucked. Brooke saw stars.

"Oh my God."

"Mmm-hmm," he hummed against her flesh, and she shuddered from head to toe as pleasure rolled through her.

"Cade. Oh, Cade. I can't believe you wanted to be a priest. I am *so* thankful you changed your mind."

He laughed as his tongue flicked her nipple before he let it pop out of his mouth again. "Seriously, angel, all I've done is suck your pretty nipple. Don't be happy yet that I'm not a priest."

She put her fingers into his hair, pulled his head back down again. "I'm happy. Very happy. Keep going."

"If this makes you happy, I can't wait to see what happens when I slide my tongue into your hot little body."

Brooke's breath caught in her throat. How was she going to survive it when he did that?

He sucked her nipples, alternating between them, holding her high as he did so while she mewed and held his dark head to her body. Finally he dropped her down and stabbed his tongue into her mouth.

"Cade," she moaned between kisses. "Why did I wait for this?"

"I don't know, angel. But I'm going to make up for lost time, promise."

He tipped her backward then, lowering her to the bed and coming down on top of her. He hesitated for a moment, and she opened her eyes to find him looking at her with a serious expression.

"You okay?"

She nodded. "It's you, Cade. I'm fine."

He smoothed a hand down her chest, over her breasts, down her abdomen. She tensed a little when he reached the waistband of her G-string. He didn't miss it.

"I won't touch you there if you don't want me to."

"I want you to. I honestly do. It's muscle memory, I think."

"We're going slowly here," he said, teasing the top of her panties. And then he dropped down to that level and ran his tongue along the line of her waistband.

Brooke clutched his head, squeezing her fingers in his hair, her heart hammering harder than she would have thought possible. This wasn't her first time with a man, wasn't her first time having a man perform oral sex on her, but this was definitely her first time being in love with the man doing it.

He rose over her and pulled her panties down her hips, down her thighs, and then dropped them on the night table.

"Gorgeous," he said, staring at her nakedness. "Everything I dreamed you'd be."

He skimmed his fingers over her mound, gently.

When she'd started texting with him, she'd trimmed and shaved because it made her feel sexy. She was glad she'd done it now, because his fingers on her, gliding over bare skin the lower he went, was erotic and exciting.

"You're bare down here. I like it. May I?"

She couldn't have loved him more than when he asked the question. "Yes."

He slid a finger over her clit, between her labia, down through the wetness he'd created. But he didn't try to put his finger inside her. He just dipped and swirled and rubbed around her clit while she bit her lip and clutched fistfuls of covers in her hands.

"I want to lick you here," he said, skimming his thumb over her clit again, setting up a cascade of sensation inside her body.

"I want that so badly."

He dropped his shoulders between her legs, and she widened them to accommodate him. Butterflies fluttered in her stomach at the way he looked between her legs, this big man getting ready to touch his mouth to her body in a place that hadn't felt that kind of sensation for far too long.

He spread her with his thumbs and then dropped until he was almost there. He shot her a grin. "You ready?"

She could only nod.

"Pinch your nipples, angel. I want to watch you do that while I lick you."

Heat flared beneath her skin, but she did as he said, her body zinging with sparks as she pinched.

And then his tongue dropped into her heat and she arched her back up off the bed, crying out.

It was too much pleasure, too much anticipation, too much sensation all at once.

But that didn't stop him. He swirled his tongue over her clit, down between her lips, inside her, back up again. Over and over he licked and retreated, licked and retreated, until the tension building inside her was at a fever pitch.

"I want to add a finger, angel. Will you let me do that?"

"Yes. Anything you want. Please."

He sucked her clit between his lips and slid a finger inside her at the same time. Brooke exploded, crying out, her body shaking as her orgasm rippled through her.

His finger didn't retreat, and she didn't want it to. Instead, he'd found her G-spot, that sensitive area inside that he stroked as she came.

Brooke nearly blacked out the pleasure was so insane. But she held on to her consciousness and carefully floated back to herself, becoming aware that he'd stopped applying direct stimulation to her oversensitive flesh. He was stroking the insides of her thighs, licking around her clit without touching it, calming her while also keeping her ready for more.

She touched his head, stroked his hair, his ear. "You're too good to be true, Cade Rodgers with a *D*," she said, trying to be lighthearted when she was feeling anything but.

No, she was feeling as if her world had been thrown

into a new kind of chaos. A good kind of chaos, at least where it involved Cade, but chaos nonetheless.

"I'm *very* glad you didn't become a priest," she added. "I'd be in danger of eternal damnation for corrupting you if you had."

He laughed then. "If I were a priest, I don't think we'd have met. So you'd be safe."

"Maybe," she said. "Though maybe we'd have met anyway."

"Thankfully we don't have to worry about it." He swiped his tongue over her clit and she gasped. "We're here, now, and you are currently my favorite thing to eat."

"I want to do the same to you, Cade."

He lifted an eyebrow. "Do you?"

"Yes. I've been dying to see you since you sent me that first picture. And I've wanted to touch your eggplant since the first time you described it to me."

He snorted. "My eggplant is more than ready. But what I really want is to be inside you, Brooke. Not sure I'd last all that long if you started sucking me."

"Only one way to find out. Please," she added.

He hesitated for a long moment and then got to his feet and unbuttoned his jeans. "No finishing me, Brooke. If I tell you to stop, stop."

She briefly considered ignoring him and then realized that she owed him the same respect he'd shown her. Even if it was for a different reason, stop was stop.

"I will."

He shoved his jeans down his legs and his cock sprang free.

"Wow," she said. Cade was big, hard, and long. She'd thought there was a lot in his jeans, but she'd never really been sure. Now she knew. "You didn't quite give me the whole picture when you described it."

He wrapped his hand around it, which was an even more beautiful sight than his dick alone. She imagined him stroking it while she watched, imagined the explosion when he came.

She scrambled up onto her knees and came to the edge of the bed. He looked a little uncertain.

"You sure about this?"

"I'm not a virgin, Cade. I know what to do."

"I know that. But are you ready for it, or do you think maybe you're taking this too far too soon?"

She reached for his hips, forced him closer. Then she stuck out her tongue and licked the tip, caught the salty drop of precome that resided there.

"I've dreamed about this for weeks, imagined it in detail. It's not too soon. It's just right."

Chapter 16

Brooke opened her mouth and took him inside, and Cade stiffened. Her tongue stroked along the underside of his cock as she wrapped a hand around him and began to squeeze and caress him in rhythm.

He put a hand on her head, tangled his fingers in her hair. Gently, of course. She gazed up at him for a second with those pretty eyes and then dropped her lashes again and concentrated on what she was doing.

And wow was she doing it well. It took everything he had not to thrust into her mouth, but he locked his legs and stood still while she licked and sucked, caressing his balls with one hand while jerking him off with the other.

He'd gotten plenty of head, sometimes in times and places that were totally inappropriate, but none of it gave him the rush this moment did. Brooke Sullivan, tiny Brooke with her golden hair and lush tits and wounded eyes, was naked in front of him, sucking his dick while he still had her taste on his tongue.

Pressure began to gather in his balls, which tightened almost painfully as the base of his spine started to tingle. Explosion was imminent, and there was no way he planned to finish like this. Hell, he'd never expected any of it—not a kiss, not a taste, not her mouth on him, nothing. He wasn't wasting this chance. Just in case she came to her senses and decided there wasn't going to be another one.

"Stop," he told her, his voice hoarse as he did so.

His dick popped out of her mouth, wet and glistening, and he shuddered with the force of the desire swelling and rushing through him.

"I want you, Brooke. Want to be in you—is that going to work for you?"

She smiled softly. "I want that too."

"Need a condom," he muttered, planning to get one out of his backpack—and hoping it didn't kill the mood while he rummaged.

"I'm on the pill," she said. "And I'm clean. I haven't been with a man since before..." She swallowed and his heart throbbed. "Well, since before I was kidnapped."

Holy hell.

"I'm clean too. I never have sex without a condom —and I've grown tired of hookups, so I haven't had any in a while. But you have every right to demand I wear one, Brooke. That way you can be certain."

She pushed back on the bed until she was propped on her elbows, legs spread just enough he could see a hint of pink, and smiled.

"I am certain, Cade. Your teammates call you Saint, for goodness' sake. I have to believe they have

159

more reasons than just your onetime desire to be a priest."

"Maybe they call me that because it's ironic," he growled. "You ever think of that?"

Because he wouldn't just let her blindly think he was a good guy. That he didn't have dirty thoughts and ulterior motives of his own. He had a ton of dirty thoughts where she was concerned—and his motives weren't pure either.

He wanted her for himself. He wanted to own her body and command her pleasure. He wanted to make her so hot for him that she couldn't think straight, and he wanted to be the one to give her relief from the pain of her arousal.

She blinked, and he asked himself what the fuck he was doing. *Why put doubts in her mind, asshole?*

But she shook her head, her blond hair flying. "No, I don't think that at all. You're a saint because you have patience and understanding, Cade. That's what I see. That's what you've shown me."

She shifted her weight onto one elbow and let the other hand trail down her body, down into her wetness and heat. "Please, Cade. I want you here. Now."

Hell, there was no way he could resist that invitation. He dropped to his knees, bent over her and licked her nipples while she gasped. Then he caught her hand and sucked on the fingers she'd used to play with herself.

"Cade," she whispered, and he knew then that he would do anything to hear his name on her lips in that sweet tone.

He kissed her deeply, hotly, sinking down on her

body by degrees. And then he stopped and held himself above her, searching her gaze.

"Do you want to be on top? Is this too much?"

Her arms wrapped around his neck, her legs around his waist. "No, it's not too much. It's you and me and it's perfect."

Damn if she didn't get him right in the feels. Because he knew she hadn't trusted anyone with her body in two years, that she'd fought her demons for so long. He knew she wasn't magically over that incident, but the fact she was here, beneath him, letting the connection between them take her where it wanted to go—well, he was gutted by it. Humbled.

He didn't tell her to use the word *stop*. She already knew. Instead, he wrapped a hand around his dick and glided it through her wetness, up and down, coating himself in her moisture and hitting her clit at the same time.

He knew she liked it by the way she gasped and wriggled her hips to get closer to him. Finally he positioned himself at her entrance and pushed forward as slowly as he could manage.

Sweat broke out on his forehead. His balls ached. Brooke's breath shortened and he stopped, worried. But that wasn't panic on her face. It was bliss.

"Cade," she said again, much like before, her palm sliding along his cheek. "More. I want more."

That was the permission he needed to thrust fully inside her. She cried out and he stopped again, goose bumps cascading over his skin. It felt so good, and yet he was worried about hurting her.

Not just physically but mentally.

"You okay, angel?"

Her eyes took a moment to focus. And then she sobbed, and his world cleaved in two.

"Brooke, baby, I'm sorry," he said. "It's okay."

Emotion clogged his throat. Anger, fear, sorrow. He didn't want to hurt her, and yet he clearly had done so. He started to pull out, but her fingers curled into his arms.

"No, no. It's okay," she said through her tears, laughing now. "God, I'm sorry, I'm such a mess—but it's okay, Cade. I love—" She stopped, swallowed. "I love being with you. I'm fine. More than fine." Her eyes dropped closed for a moment. "Oh wow, so much more than fine. I thought... I thought I was dead inside, at least when it came to sex—but I'm not. I want this *so much!*"

He didn't know what to say. So he kissed her. She clung to him, and he began to move, thrusting into her, letting the pleasure lead them where it wanted. She was so wet, so tight, and his balls ached with the effort to hold on for just a little while longer.

He wanted to spend. Wanted to drive into her faster and deeper and harder until the top of his head blew off and he came powerfully within her.

But he didn't do that. He took his time, planning his thrusts, drawing out the pleasure for them both.

Brooke clung to him, her arms and legs wrapped around him, her breasts jiggling with every pump of his body into hers. Her lips were against his shoulder, her soft moans in his ear, and he felt like a king in control of the world.

He gripped her arms gently and raised them above her head. She didn't resist. Then he wrapped his fingers into hers and held her hands.

"Kiss me, angel," he said, his mouth a whisper away from hers.

Her lips met his, her tongue seeking, and Cade lost the last shreds of his control, riding her hard. Brooke thrust her hips against his, meeting him again and again.

When she cried out and stiffened beneath him, he shifted the angle of his thrusts, making sure he hit her clit with the root of his cock. She went nuclear, crying out in his ear, shaking beneath him, her pussy tightening around him as her interior muscles rippled with her orgasm.

"Cade! Oh God—Cade!"

It was all he needed to dive over the edge. His release ripped through his balls, up his shaft, exploding into a hot current inside her. Cade rode the wave until he was spent, and then he sank, panting and sweating, beside her.

He was stunned by the sheer power of what had just happened between them. It was sex—great sex—but it was more than that too.

Before he could figure out what it meant, Brooke reached for his hand. Their fingers tangled. She squeezed. He squeezed back.

"Thank you," she said softly.

"There's nothing to thank me for."

She propped herself on an elbow and gazed down at

him. Her skin was shiny with perspiration and glowing with sex.

"I think there is. You gave me back something I thought I'd lost. I'll always be grateful."

He put an arm around her and dragged her down to his chest, kissing the top of her head while she spread her fingers over his pecs and sighed.

"That sounded like goodbye, angel."

And if it was goodbye, he was going to be wrecked for a while.

"No," she whispered against his skin. "Once was not enough."

He laughed with relief as he hugged her to him. "No, it definitely wasn't."

BROOKE WAS DAZED, but in a good way. Her emotions were high, but she worked not to cry again. She'd sobbed when he'd first entered her because she'd been overcome. Sometimes she'd thought she was irreparably damaged. That she would never have sex again.

But Cade had forced her to confront that notion. Because she'd been sexually attracted to him from the first, and when they'd begun texting each other naughty words and images, she'd always dreamed it was him taking her to climax when she'd gotten herself off.

She was sore but in a good way. Cade was a big man. Even if they didn't do it again, she would know she'd been intimate with him for days. She liked the feeling, that full, slightly sore sensation that told her she'd had great sex with a partner who knew how to use what he had.

She wanted to cling to him all night long, and then she wanted to do everything again. And again.

"You want me to let Max out?" His voice was a delicious rumble in her ear.

"Yes, please."

Cade extracted himself and went to open the bathroom door. Max trotted out and came over to where Brooke lay with her hand stretched out for him. His ears perked up and he whined a little as she scratched him.

"It's okay, Max," Cade said, climbing back into bed with her. "I won't hurt her."

He put his arm over her and scratched Max's head too. The dog snorted at them both and then went to the small couch and jumped on it. After a couple of spins, he lay down and put his head on his paws.

"He's used to sleeping in bed with me," Brooke said, feeling bad about her dog having to sleep on the couch.

"Bed's too small," Cade said, his voice sounding sleepy. "Next time we'll find a king and let him join us—after the sex, I mean."

Brooke snorted. "Uh, yeah. Without a doubt."

"You say that, but I had a teammate once who dated a girl with a Pomeranian. Damn thing lay on her pillow while they fucked. Got judgy about it too."

Brooke laughed as she snuggled into his body. "How so?"

"Growled with every thrust, or so Jonah said."

"That's ridiculous."

"That's what I said. Told him he needed to stop having sex with her until she agreed to move the dog."

"And did it work?"

"Nope. He married her. For all I know, the dog is still on the pillow, judging the hell out of him. Too much pressure for me, I gotta say."

Brooke couldn't help but snort a laugh. "You're making that up."

"I'm not, angel. Swear it."

She laid an arm across him and sighed. He was warm to the touch. She liked touching him now that she'd crossed that barrier.

"I don't want Max judging you. Or me, I should add. He can go in another room when we get sexy together."

"He can stay so long as he minds his own business," Cade said with a laugh. He trailed his fingers up and down her arm. "You sure you're okay after that?"

She pushed up on an elbow to gaze down at him. "The truth?"

"Yep."

"I'm a bit sore. You aren't a little guy, Cade Rodgers with a *D*. But it was amazing, and I want to do it again. Soon."

He arched an eyebrow. "How soon?"

She glanced down the luscious expanse of his flat abdomen. His dick was half hard already and her belly knotted in anticipation. "Five minutes?"

"How about now, angel? You climb up here and put that lovely pussy in my face. Guarantee I'll be ready once I make you come with my tongue again."

Brooke shivered at the thought. And then she got an idea. "Okay. But only if I get to do you at the same time."

He closed his eyes. "Fuck, I died and went to heaven. Get up here, angel. I want to make you scream."

"Just so long as you know I intend to make you scream too."

"Deal."

Chapter 17

He didn't scream, but he damn sure groaned. And though he didn't want to, he ended up coming in her throat. Not that she made any moves to let him go when it happened. Brooke fastened her mouth around him and drank him in while he tried to remember how to breathe.

When it was over, when he was spent and limp, he still managed to flip her over and devour her with his lips and teeth and tongue until she clutched his head and moaned. "Oh Cade. *Cade... Yes, yes, yes...*"

They fell asleep in each other's arms, exhausted but happy. Max slept too. Cade woke up a couple of times, but everything was quiet and still. Brooke slept wedged against him. Some women moved as soon as they wanted to sleep, but not Brooke. She curled into his body and stayed there.

Each time he woke, she was still there. Maybe flipped, but still pressed to him. He didn't mind. In fact, he took the opportunity to touch her. He toyed with her nipples, skimmed his fingers down her belly and over her mound. She made noises, but she didn't try to move away. No, she tried to move toward him.

He thought about dropping between her legs and licking her into another orgasm, but she needed the sleep, so he didn't actually disturb her. There would, hopefully, be plenty of time for more hot sex together now that they'd smashed that barrier.

He woke for the last time around six thirty. Later than he usually did, but considering last night's departure from her place and then the totally unexpected sexual encounters, he'd had a long day yesterday.

Brooke still slept. Max was asleep as well, though he'd wake in a heartbeat if Cade moved. The dog had been really good throughout the night, but the motel was fairly quiet and nothing had disturbed him enough to bark.

Cade reached for his phone and checked his texts. There were messages from Hacker telling him to call when he could. If it had been urgent, Hacker would have said, so Cade didn't worry about waiting. When Brooke woke or Max wanted out, Cade would call back.

He had no doubt his teammate was on top of things. Hacker was an interesting dude. He didn't talk about himself much, but it was clear he came from a moneyed background. The dude had monogrammed cuffs, which Cade had discovered at one of the weddings they'd been at. Cade had never seen monogrammed cuffs before. Hacker also wore cuff links, and his blazer had gold buttons on the sleeves. He drank red wine, and once when Cade had called him at home, he'd heard opera in the background.

Hacker had gone to college, but he'd dropped out before completing a degree or he'd likely be an officer. What made a guy like that decide to be a grunt—and not just any grunt, but a Special Operator, which meant there'd been a lot of hard training and deprivation along the way—was beyond Cade.

For him, the choice had been an easy one. Growing up in the Mississippi Delta with a mother who worked two jobs just to get by and knowing he'd never be able to go to college or likely do anything beyond getting a job at the local garage, the military had been a no-brainer. Three squares a day, a roof over your head, medical care, and a paycheck along with the promise of college?

Yep, he'd signed up and hadn't looked back. That he'd ended up in HOT was a bonus he hadn't planned on. Turned out he was good at fighting battles, and he was relentlessly cool in the face of danger. He'd wanted Delta Force, but when he'd learned of the existence of HOT, he'd wanted that even more. It had taken a lot of hard work, but he'd gotten command of his own squad eventually. Echo was all his, and he took pride in leading his guys through thick and thin.

Brooke turned in her sleep, presenting her back to him. The covers inched down until her spine was exposed. He pushed them down even more, until he could see her naked ass.

Such a pretty ass. He wanted to gather it in both hands and hold it while he thrust inside her and made them both come.

He put an arm around her and pulled her close, her back to his front, content to just hold her until she woke. She made a soft sound in her throat, and then she wiggled her shapely rear against him.

He reached up to cup a breast, and she made that sound again.

"You're awake, aren't you?" he murmured as he pinched her nipple.

"Getting there. Mmm, somebody's hard."

"Somebody definitely is." He kissed her shoulder. "You up for a little fun?"

"So long as that fun involves you inside me, yes, I am."

He skimmed his fingers down her side, around to the back of her thigh. "You want to turn over or see where we get this way?"

He had to ask her these things because he didn't want to scare her. If she were anyone else, he'd take the lead and do what he wanted, knowing that her pleasure was foremost in his mind and that the end result would be good for her.

"Do what you want, Cade. I trust you."

His heart squeezed hard at those words. She trusted him, and he didn't take that lightly. He was honored, of course. But he also wanted to growl and claim her as his to anyone who dared to think differently.

His woman. *His* lover. His to protect and cherish and give multiple orgasms to.

He urged her thighs up and out of the way so that she was practically clasping her knees, and then he skated his fingers through her wetness. She was hot and silky, and he nearly groaned at the feel of her.

Cade grasped his cock and pushed it into all that heat and liquid heaven. "God, you feel good," he told her. "So perfect."

"So do you."

He wanted to thrust quickly until he came, but he was mindful of what she'd said about being sore last night. So he moved slowly, deliberately, pulling all the way out before gliding in again.

He hooked an arm around one of her thighs, spreading her wide. Then he found her clit and strummed it like a fine instrument while he continued to slide into her. She gasped and shook—and then she cried out, her body trembling as a climax ripped through her.

He let her leg go, kissed her shoulder while she dragged in first one breath and then another.

"Oh, wow, I missed that," she finally said when she'd come back down to earth, his tongue still on her shoulder and his cock still deep inside her.

He didn't like to think about her doing this with anyone else. About another man giving her pleasure.

"Then you need more," he told her. He pushed her onto her stomach, prepared to stop if she protested or showed any fear at the movement, but she didn't.

He withdrew from her body, lifted her hips, tucked a pillow beneath them, and grasped her waist as he knelt behind her. "You okay?"

"I will be when you make me come again."

That was all he needed to push inside her and start

moving, riding her gently at first and then harder as need overtook him. She came again quickly, meeting his thrusts with equal force, stiffening as the wave crashed over her.

Cade didn't have time to marvel at her response because his own crisis grabbed hold of his balls and didn't let go until he was utterly drained, groaning as he came so hard he saw stars. They collapsed on the bed together, a tangle of sweaty limbs and labored breaths.

Cade rolled away to give her space. Brooke turned over, lying with her eyes closed and her luscious body on full display. He devoured her with his gaze, taking in her small, perfect body with big tits, wide hips, and a glistening pussy that he wanted to taste again. Her belly was flat but also soft. Not hard like his, but smooth and soft like someone who worked out but didn't deprive herself of food.

"I love being with you, Cade," she said finally, though she didn't open her eyes. "I'm sorry I kept you at a distance for so long. I'm sorry it took something like this to let you into my life for real."

"Two weeks isn't all that long. We were still getting to know each other."

"I know."

He rolled to his side and fondled her nipples. She sighed. "Be truthful with me, Brooke."

Her eyes snapped open, her baby blues meeting his gaze. She looked wary. "I have been."

"I know that, angel. But I want you to be truthful with yourself too. You experienced a trauma two years ago. You aren't suddenly cured because we've had sex. You still need to process it."

Her lashes dropped over her eyes. "I'm fine. I feel great."

He sighed. "Baby. Promise me."

She reached up and ran her palm along his jaw. "I promise to see my therapist. I promise to tell her what really happened two years ago."

He dipped his mouth to hers and kissed her. "I'm glad. Because I want to keep doing this with you, Brooke. I want to move forward with you, and I don't want anything to stop that from happening."

"It won't," she said.

He wasn't sure he believed her.

CADE GOT up and dragged jeans on over his naked body, then pulled a T-shirt over his head and scrubbed his hands through his hair. Brooke watched in awe. She didn't think she'd ever seen a sexier man than Cade Rodgers.

He was comfortable with himself, and he damn sure knew his way around a woman's body. His tongue should be a registered weapon. His cock—damn, his cock ought to be licensed as a clear and present danger to her peace of mind. She'd been with other men, but she'd never wanted to get *that* acquainted with their cocks.

Cade's, however… Well, she could spend a lot of time licking him like a lollipop and never grow tired of doing so. Most dicks were not memorable. Most were unattractive. But if Cade sent her a dick pic, she'd make it into her wallpaper.

Okay, maybe not her wallpaper. Decency standards and all. But she'd damn sure use it to get herself off when he wasn't around.

"You want to go out, Max?"

Max jumped off the couch and did a few whirls. Then he barked.

"Hey," Brooke said. "No barking."

Max woofed more quietly the next time. Cade laughed as he grabbed the leash. "Be thinking about what you want for breakfast," he said as he clipped on the leash.

"Your cock," she said automatically.

Cade's nostrils flared. "Angel."

She didn't know who the hell she was turning into, but she trailed her fingers down her abdomen and into the wetness below. "I'm going to shower. Maybe you can join me?"

"How many times can you…?" He shook his head. "Yeah, I want to join you. Gotta take the dog out first."

"Better hurry."

SHE'D JUST TURNED on the shower when Cade returned. She was standing in the bathroom, utterly naked, when he came inside and looked at her with that intense *I'm going to fuck you* look he had.

He stripped out of his clothes and left them where

175

they landed. Then he picked her up and she wrapped her legs around him. He made her feel like she weighed next to nothing as he stepped into the shower with her.

It was a small shower, the water tolerably warm but nothing to write home about. The tub was actually porcelain, a holdover from days gone by, and the shower head sprayed an anemic stream of water on them.

He backed her into it, fused his mouth to hers. Brooke threaded her arms around his neck and kissed him for all she was worth.

No, in some ways she didn't recognize the person she was with him. But in others, she knew she was who she was supposed to be. Who she would have been without the trauma of her past.

He lifted her up and then brought her down on his stone-hard cock. Brooke gasped as he filled her. She weighed nothing in his arms. Absolutely nothing.

He held her with one arm beneath her ass, lifting her again and again as he fucked her, his other hand on her breasts, pinching her nipples. Brooke clung to him, let him take her where he wanted, knowing it would be good for them both if she gave up control.

She was sore, and she was happy. Cade drove himself home inside her until she caught fire and came in one long, shuddering moan that seemed to go on forever. She could tell when he came because he finally pushed her back against the wall and ground his hips into her, grunting when his climax hit him.

When it was over, he helped her wash, helped her remove the semen that dripped down her thighs, and then he washed her hair and rinsed it for her. She spent far more time than she should soaping his body, exploring the hard muscles, until finally he took her hand and peeled the sponge out of it.

"No more," he told her. "Not this time."

They finished their shower, then got out and dressed, exchanging kisses as they did so. It was such a normal thing, other than the cheap hotel room, and it made Brooke's heart sing.

She was in love with this man, for the first time in her life, and she wanted to keep feeling this way. She didn't want to think about the past or about Scott and the man in the corridor, but she knew those things were waiting for her. They hadn't gone away at all.

After they dressed, Cade tucked his weapons into the holsters he'd secreted on his body. She watched him do it, her heart throbbing. This was his life. Guns. Violence. Danger.

It scared her. What if something happened to him?

"Breakfast?" he asked her when he was done.

She nodded, her throat tight, her mind still caught in the grip of her fear for him.

He tilted his head. "Something wrong?"

"No, nothing."

His brows drew together. "Don't lie to me, angel. It's the guns, isn't it?"

"It's what you do. I know that. I just worry."

"Don't worry. I'm the nightmare standing between you and those who would harm you. Never forget that."

Her stomach trembled inside. "I won't."

His phone rang before he could say anything else. "Yeah."

Brooke watched his expression harden, his jaw tighten, and her nerves popped like a high-tension line. His gaze lifted to her, his brows drawing down.

"We'll be there in an hour."

"What's wrong?" she asked when he dropped his arm to his side.

He didn't stop frowning. "Bert's daughter has been abducted."

Brooke blinked. "Bert? Bert Lewis, the security guard at my building?" Logically, she knew that's who he meant, but she was having trouble processing it. Who would abduct Bert's little girl?

"Yes, that Bert."

Her stomach twisted before falling into her toes. "Oh my God, what happened? Who took Amy? Why would they go after her?"

He came over and put his hands on her shoulders, ran them down her arms. It soothed her, but barely.

"There's no easy way to say this, angel." He hesitated. "The Espinoza Cartel—those are the men that Scott was selling weapons to—they're the ones who took her."

Chapter 18

"It's my fault. They were after me, weren't they?"

Fury rolled deep inside him. "It's not your fault. It's Scott Lloyd's fault. Don't ever forget that."

"But what does Bert or his child have to do with any of this? What can these people expect to happen now?"

He held her by the shoulders, wishing he could take away her pain and fear. She trembled. "I don't know, angel. But we've got to go to HQ and find out what happens next. We'll get Bert's daughter back—but first we need to know what they want, and we need a plan."

She nodded as if she trusted him to solve the problem completely. "You can't let anything happen to her. Amy is Bert's life. He and his wife tried for so long to have her—they'd given up hope when Shelly got pregnant. Amy is their only child."

Usually he walled off his emotions and got the job done. It was as natural as breathing. But this time—

Hell, this time he was pissed. He didn't know what those fuckers wanted, but if they were abducting little girls, they were soulless monsters who would stop at nothing.

He intended to stop them though. Stop them cold before they hurt Amy. And before they could harm Brooke. Because he had no doubt this somehow related to Brooke and what she might know or might have seen.

"Let's get going," he told her.

She nodded and turned away to get her bags. They loaded everything in his truck and then hit a drive-through for a quick bite and some coffee. He bought a small breakfast sandwich for Max too.

Brooke didn't appear to notice him order it, but she found it when she was rummaging through the bag for their breakfast. "Is this yours?" she asked, holding it up.

"Nope. Thought Max needed something too."

She snorted. "Oh, Cade. My dog is going to weigh two hundred pounds when you're done if I don't watch you closely."

He glanced in the rearview. Max sat back against the seat, belted in with his special seat belt, and watched them both.

"Look at that face," Cade said. "How can you resist it?"

Brooke sighed as she unwrapped the sandwich. "I can't. Guess you can't either."

She fed Max and then sat back and sighed, sipping her coffee as the miles went by. He knew she was probably thinking of her own treatment at the hands of her kidnappers and worrying for Amy. He wanted to take that fear away from her, but he couldn't.

"I'm sorry, angel," he said after a while. "I know this hurts."

It was a good hour's drive from the motel in southern Maryland to HOT HQ, and she hadn't said anything for the past twenty minutes as she'd stared out the window and drank her coffee.

He was beginning to feel a little desperate, truth be told. Last night—and this morning—had been so perfect, so earth-shattering, that he didn't want to go back to the way it was before.

There was something about this woman that made him crazy. Crazy hot, crazy horny, crazy for her in general. He'd never felt like this before. He didn't quite understand how or why, but she meant something to him. Something more than anyone else he'd ever been with.

She turned to gaze at him. There were worry lines on her forehead. "I keep reminding myself that Scott is the one who got involved with a drug cartel in the first place. He's the one who decided to sell them weapons."

"Yeah. I wish I'd seen this one coming last night. I could have protected Bert's little girl."

"You couldn't know."

No, he couldn't have. He'd gotten Brooke out of there, but he'd never thought the cartel would go after someone else. They must have had the building under surveillance for quite some time. Someone had helped them erase the recordings. Had it been Bert? Was he involved in helping the cartel's man enter the building, undetected by security cameras? If so, why had he been so free with information when Cade had talked to him? It didn't make sense.

But Cade was also realistic enough to realize that it must have been an inside job. And Bert was as likely a candidate as any, especially now that the cartel had his daughter. Why would they have chosen her otherwise?

"We'll get her out. I promise."

"I know." She turned to gaze out the window. She was quiet, and he didn't like it. It felt like she was shutting him out, and he hated that feeling. He'd been a part of her not so long ago, his cock and his tongue and his soul, deep inside her, giving and taking and forging bonds he'd thought were more solid than they seemed at this moment.

"You don't sound like you're very confident."

She turned. "I am, Cade. I promise I am. I just… I keep thinking about Amy, all alone and scared. She's six, and she'll be terrified. If what happened to me turned my life upside down, what will happen to a kid? I'm also scared about you leaving me to go and free Amy, and I don't know how to process any of this fear I'm feeling."

"You won't be in any danger. I'll make sure of it before I go."

"That's not what I meant."

He blinked. "You're scared… *for* me?"

It hardly seemed possible, and yet there it was.

"I know I shouldn't be. Grace says goodbye to Garrett all the time, and he always comes back. And it's not like you're going alone. You go with a team."

Cade flexed his hands on the wheel. "I'm coming back, angel. Don't worry about that."

"But I do. I can't help it. I…" She sighed and raked a hand through her hair. "This thing between us is new, but I trust you. I didn't think I'd ever get past what happened to me, but sex with you… It's amazing. I don't think about some asshole abusing me when I'm with you. I think of you and us and all the things I want to do with you. All the things I feel."

He swallowed the knot in his throat. "I feel things too," he said. "And I worry about you. I don't want you anywhere near this mess right now, and yet I'm driving you into the eye of the storm. It's killing me because I'd rather take you somewhere far away from the whole damned thing."

"I guess we're both in a pickle then."

"Yeah, guess so."

"But Cade, you're only taking me to HOT HQ— don't look shocked, I know what it is after what I went through. I'm not really in any danger. I'm especially in no danger in the middle of HOT."

What she said was true, and yet he couldn't shake the gut-deep feeling he had that something was going to go wrong. That she'd be a part of this whole thing before it was over. Still, he wasn't telling her that.

"I know how you feel being around the guys. You aren't going to like it there. Too many men."

She laughed. "So you noticed that, I guess."

"It wasn't difficult. You and Grace spent the entire football game in the kitchen. Not exactly hard to connect the dots."

"Maybe I don't care about football. Maybe we were talking."

"You care about football. You have a favorite team."

"Okay, fine. But my favorite team wasn't playing, so Grace and I chatted instead."

"You freaked out the second I walked into the room. And don't think I didn't notice how tense you were when the guys all went to grab snacks during halftime. They make you uncomfortable."

"And then there was the wedding," she said. "The colonel's wedding where you must have thought I was insane."

He remembered his first sight of her that night, how gorgeous and utterly enchanting she seemed to him. He'd wanted to get to know her, but Garrett and Grace showed up and dragged her away as if he'd been planning to strip her naked and fuck her right there in public.

It had been an odd night, and he'd been left with an emptiness that had been stronger than any he usually felt. But then he'd moved on and forgotten about it— well, okay, he hadn't quite forgotten, but he'd known it wasn't ever happening the next few times he saw her.

"I didn't think that," he said. "You seemed troubled. And you weren't scared of me that night."

"I was drunk. Self-medication, Cade. I'd also taken a Xanax, which meant I was pretty loopy."

"You didn't seem loopy. You seemed… a little uninhibited, but not out of control."

"I wasn't out of control. I got pretty good at self-medicating for a while there. But I don't mix alcohol and antidepressants anymore, promise. That was a dumb idea, and I paid for it with a monster hangover."

"So why'd you do it?"

"Truthfully? I'd forgotten I'd taken the Xanax when someone handed me a drink. By the time I remembered, I'd had a mixed drink and felt fine. So I had another. And then another. I almost convinced myself that I was over my fears. In fact, when you started talking to me, I'd pretty much already determined to take one of you home that night."

Jesus, he was glad he was the one she'd talked to first. Even if Garrett and Grace hadn't interfered, he liked to think his patience and self-control would have held him back from taking advantage of her. One of the other guys would have been on her like a bee to nectar.

"As much as I woulda liked to have been the one you took home, I'm glad it didn't happen that night." Because he had no doubt he wouldn't have seen her again. It would have been sex and nothing else—and that wasn't enough with her.

"Me too." She smiled. "Last night was *so* much better than it could have been back then."

"So you gonna be all right around all these guys?"

"I'll be fine, Cade. I know they're the good guys."

SHE'D TOLD Cade she would be okay, but she was still nervous once they arrived at HOT HQ. The men were big, and many of them walked around with firearms openly strapped to their sides. There were women too, though not as many.

They had to pass through several security checks,

but when they were finally through, Cade took her to a conference room with a big table and chairs arranged around it. There were computers at every seat and a huge monitor hanging at one end of the room. There was another monitor with clocks displayed on it, showing every time zone across the world.

Cade pulled out a seat for her and she sat. "I've got to go to another area for a little bit, angel. You'll be fine here. Airman Reynolds will be with you until I return."

Her heart jumped in protest, but then the door opened and a woman in uniform walked in. Her hair was neatly contained in a bun at the base of her neck and her smile was friendly.

"You'll be back?"

He dropped a quick kiss on her lips. "I'll be back. Promise. Can you show Miss Sullivan the organizational film, Airman?" he said to the young woman standing just inside the door.

"Absolutely, sir. Be happy to." She gazed at him with something more than professional courtesy. A pinprick of jealousy stabbed into Brooke.

Mine. Hands off. Even mental hands.

Cade grinned at the woman, and Brooke's jealousy throbbed. "I'm a sergeant, not a sir."

"Yes, Sergeant."

He strode from the room and Brooke tried to breathe normally. Not because she was scared, but because he made her insides churn and her breath shorten whenever he was near. Especially when he kissed her. He made her feel like she'd gotten on a roller coaster, but she didn't want off.

Now that he was gone, the room seemed emptier. Did Grace feel terrified whenever Garrett was preparing to go into badass mode? Brooke had never asked. She felt somewhat guilty for it now. Grace was her friend and Brooke cared, but it was as if she'd put on blinders to everything Garrett did after her kidnapping.

His kidnapping too, because he'd been there, though not as long as she'd been. And he'd never looked scared. She remembered that. There'd been utter fury on his face. His gaze had been a lethal promise to the men holding them.

She didn't know what had happened that night, because they'd kept her in the van when they took him out to their meeting, but she'd been free shortly after that. There'd been men in wetsuits who smelled like vegetation and mud as they dripped water onto the ground beside her. One had thrown her over his shoulder and carried her. She'd tossed those pajamas rather than wash them, though that had more to do with the men who'd held her captive than with the one who'd gotten her wet and dirty when he'd rescued her.

Airman Reynolds tapped some keys on one of the consoles and a film came up. "It's not as exciting as anything Hollywood puts out about Special Ops, but this will give you an idea what our scope is. Though not all of it since much of the mission is classified. Feel free to ask questions during the presentation. If I can answer, I will. And if I can't, it's probably classified."

"WHY DID they take the security guard's daughter?" Cade asked the solemn crew gathered in the squad ready room. He'd come in late to the briefing, but he was catching up.

Ghost and Viper were both there too. Ghost was taking lead on this one, so Viper mostly sat silent, arms crossed, frown intact. For a man who'd so recently gotten married, it sure hadn't softened him at all. Oh, whenever Kat was around, there was a notable dulling of his sharp edges, but the man was still as intense as ever.

Then again, his wife wasn't exactly a pussycat. She might be pregnant, but you never forgot who you were dealing with when she spoke to you. The Russian operative was almost as scary as her husband. Together, they were a force to be reckoned with. If they ever decided to go into private contracting, it would be a huge loss for HOT. Not that Kat was part of the organization. So far as he knew, she was out of the business.

Ghost sighed and raked his fingers through his hair. "You want to guess, or you want me to lay it out for you?"

Cade didn't like where this was leading. "Bert's the one who let the cartel's man in. And erased the footage."

Ghost nodded. "That's right."

Anger twisted in his gut. Brooke liked Bert. Hell, he'd liked Bert. But he was trained to expect the worst out of people. Brooke, however—well, she wasn't going to take it very easily that her favorite security guard was involved.

"Why?"

Ghost shook his head, and Cade knew it was something he wasn't going to like.

"His wife was recently diagnosed with multiple sclerosis. He's facing crushing medical bills. So when Scott Lloyd asked him to let some men in a few times off the record—which meant doctoring the footage as well—he did. Because Lloyd paid him to look the other way. But then the visitors started making payments too, asking for information. You might say Bert Lewis made a deal with the devil. Once it started, he was powerless to stop it. So he kept taking the money, doctoring the footage, and looking the other way. When Lloyd was killed, he knew he'd gotten in too deep, but he didn't come forward because they'd threatened his family if he did. So far as we can tell, he didn't know that Andreas Lopez was there to kill Lloyd that night. He only figured it out once a neighbor called the front desk when Brooke's dog kept barking."

"Jesus," Cade said. "So what happened to make them take his kid anyway? Did he talk?" Except if he had, the cartel would have killed him and his family. Their bodies would be at the bottom of the Chesapeake by now.

"No, he didn't talk. But Scott Lloyd apparently didn't deliver on the last shipment. The cartel wants to know where those weapons are, and they're leaning hard on anyone with a connection to Lloyd."

"How the hell would Bert know what Lloyd did with the shipment?"

"He doesn't," Mendez interjected. "Lloyd kept records, but they're missing. He erased everything from his computers, but there was a copy made before he did that."

Cade didn't even have to ask how they knew. He glanced at Hacker, who winked.

"And they think Bert has the copy?"

"I think they know he doesn't by now. But they wanted to give him incentive to get it, so they took his daughter."

"I guess someone has a theory about who has the copy," Cade said, though the stone in his gut told him he knew the name they were all looking for.

"Scott Lloyd was obsessed with Brooke Sullivan," Ghost said, bringing up a file on the computer that displayed on the screen at the front of the room. "He planned to marry her. He had an entire file that was all about her—photos, details about her life, details about their dates. He kept a journal, and in it he wrote how he knew she wasn't in love with him but he was convinced it would all change if he could offer her a new life."

There were pictures of Brooke that she couldn't have known were taken. Her striding out of the building with Max, her blond hair in a ponytail. Her in a nice dress, sitting on Scott Lloyd's couch, drink in hand. Scott was there beside her, holding his own drink. The picture was taken in such a way she wouldn't have known he'd been snapping photos with a remote camera.

She was beautiful and vulnerable, and Cade wanted to sweep her into his arms and hold her close. His anger glowed hot at the invasion of her privacy, and also at the fact Scott had used her to excuse his criminal activities. "So he blamed Brooke for his bad choices?"

"He certainly used her to justify them. But I think we all know he would have done those things anyway. Clearly he went to work for Black Eagle and started fudging the books pretty quickly. He didn't work alone though. The ATF has been investigating irregularities at Black Eagle for quite some time. They have an informant there, and he claims that Lloyd was only following orders. But Lloyd tried to make his own deals outside of channels, so he was pissing off both the Espinoza Cartel and his bosses at Black Eagle. The last shipment he was supposed to deliver never arrived. It's not in BE's Brazilian warehouses either, which is where the guns were manufactured."

"How many guns?"

"Ten thousand."

Somebody whistled.

"You can't just hide ten thousand guns. They'd make a pretty big pile somewhere."

"They would indeed," Mendez interjected. "And we're going to find them. Last thing we need is that many weapons in the hands of the Espinozas so they can sell them on the black market." He stood upright from where he'd been leaning against a table, arms and legs crossed. "Either we find them the easy way, which is by finding the copy Scott Lloyd made of his records, or we find them the hard way."

Cade knew what that meant. They all did. A team—

probably Echo Squad—in Brazil, tracing the shipment to the last known point.

"Since I'm sure we all want the easy way," Ghost continued, "we're going to need to talk to Miss Sullivan. So how about we take this little party to her and find out what she knows?"

Chapter 19

"I... I don't have anything," Brooke said, breathing evenly as she gazed up at the big men standing over her in the conference room. "Scott never gave me anything to hold for him."

She'd been watching the film that Airman Reynolds put on for her when the doors had opened and a group of men came striding in. They were big. Lethal. She knew them all, however, because she'd either met them at Grace's or she'd seen them at Buddy's Bar & Grill on the rare occasions she'd gone there at Grace's request.

Yes, they were big and scary—but she wasn't as scared as she'd expected. She glanced at Cade, and her heart felt happy instead of anxious. He gave her strength. She knew that now. She smiled to let him know she was fine. Because she could see the hint of worry on his features, and she wanted him to know it was okay. *She* was okay.

"He hasn't given you anything in the past few days?

Did you get any unexpected mail?" Lieutenant Colonel Bishop asked. *Ghost*, she thought. *They call him Ghost.*

She pictured her desk and all the packages from clients and companies. She had a ton of unopened sample boxes she'd been meaning to get to—but they weren't from Scott.

"Nothing unexpected, no." The last thing she'd gotten had been a package the day she'd found Scott's body. She hadn't opened it, but it was from a company she'd been expecting stuff from. She'd gotten a call from the front desk, she'd gone downstairs—and come back to find Scott in front of her door. "Wait, yes, he gave me something. But it was just some books I loaned to him a while back. It was, uh, the day I found him."

The men exchanged glances.

"Did you happen to look inside those books at all, Miss Sullivan?" Ghost asked.

"No. I put the bag on the bookshelf, I think. I didn't take the books out. I would have put them away that evening, but I never got around to it because I found Scott on the floor. They should still be on the shelf. Or by the chair. Maybe." She thought about Scott handing her the bag, her walking inside her condo, Max whirling… "Wait, no, they're still on the entry table. I never got the chance to put them away."

"What kind of bag?"

"A white plastic bag."

"Titles?"

She had to think about it. "I only remember two of them." She rattled them off. That seemed to be good enough for the colonel.

"I'm going to need to send someone to your apartment to retrieve those books, Miss Sullivan. Is that okay with you?"

She nodded. "Yes, of course. Do you think he put something in one of the books?"

"It's hard to say for certain, but it's possible." He said a few more things, things that were hard to process about Scott and his feelings for her. *Obsessed* was the word that stuck in her head. Brooke couldn't process it. Not right now.

"What about Amy?" she asked, because she couldn't forget that Bert's little girl was being held somewhere by bad men who would hurt her if they didn't get what they wanted. "When will you rescue her?"

"We have to find where they're holding her, but as soon as we know that, we'll get her."

Anxiety flared in her belly. "You can't let them keep her. She's probably scared out of her mind. And then there are her parents. They must be beside themselves."

"We're working on it, Miss Sullivan," Ghost said. "I promise you, we'll get her just as quickly as we can. If you'll excuse us now, we have a lot of work to do."

Brooke knew when she'd been dismissed. She wanted to tell this arrogant man where to shove it, but she also knew that he wouldn't react. And that would be more infuriating than his dismissal.

Cade winked as he walked out with the others. She was annoyed at everything, and yet happiness glowed inside her at his look. Oh yeah, she was so gone over that man. But how did he feel?

BROOKE ATTACKED the dough with a vengeance. Grace sat at the kitchen island and watched her, a slightly bemused look on her face.

"You planning to kill the dough or make biscuits?"

Brooke blew out a breath, ruffling the hair that had fallen into her face. "I'm making biscuits."

"You're angry."

"Not angry. Worried. Frustrated. Feeling itchy and edgy and all kinds of things I don't even understand."

"So…," Grace said, lifting an eyebrow. "You and Saint, huh?"

The surge of warmth and happiness she'd grown used to feeling at the thought of Cade flooded her as usual. She smiled at her friend. Cade had brought her over to Grace's and dropped her off over an hour ago. She'd wanted to climb him and kiss him and fuck his brains out all at the same time.

"Yeah. Silly, right?"

Grace shook her head. "Not at all. I told you these guys are lethal to our resistance. But honey, are you sure you're ready for this?"

There was a pinprick of annoyance in her soul. But she understood where her bestie was coming from. "Even if I'm not, it's too late. I'm in love with him."

Grace's eyebrows rose. "You're sure? You haven't known him all that long."

Brooke rolled out the dough and gave her friend a significant look. "Seriously? You were with Garrett for how long before you fell for him?"

"About forty-eight hours," Grace mumbled.

"Exactly."

Grace ran her finger around the rim of her glass. She drank grape juice while Brooke had a barely touched glass of wine sitting nearby. "But honey... do you know how he feels?"

Brooke frowned because that right there was the fly in her soup. She had no idea how Cade felt. He hadn't said. To be fair, she hadn't told him either. They'd said things to each other about how this was different from anything they'd felt before, but they hadn't quite taken the leap to actually declaring their love.

So maybe he didn't love her at all. Maybe he felt responsible for her in a way. Maybe he was giving her what she wanted in the hopes of healing her, but his feelings weren't engaged the same as hers.

She had no idea. Maybe she should have said something to him when he'd kissed her in his truck before delivering her to Grace.

"I know he cares," she said and then felt like an idiot. It was such a nonanswer. The kind a lovestruck girl gave when she had no idea if the man she was obsessed with felt one-tenth the same.

"That's good," Grace said softly, and Brooke knew her friend was trying not to say what she really wanted to say.

"Just say it, Gracie," Brooke told her.

"There's nothing to say. I just hope he feels the same as you do. Because you deserve a man who's crazy for you and treats you right."

As opposed to a man who was just crazy for her but

didn't care what she wanted. She was still reeling from the revelation that Scott had been obsessed with her. *Obsessed* was the word Ghost had used, and she'd been turning it over in her head ever since. Cade hadn't contradicted it when she'd looked to him for reassurance. On the ride over here, she'd asked him what Ghost had meant.

"Scott Lloyd was convinced you were his soul mate, I think. He was planning to ask you to marry him at some point."

Brooke hadn't understood it at all. She'd never given Scott any hints she felt anything for him. But she had gone on more than one date, though she'd known after the first one that nothing was going to happen. When she'd said that to Cade, he'd told her to stop.

"It's not your fault, Brooke. None of this is your fault. He made bad choices, and he made choices that he tried to justify to himself by using you as an object to be acquired—but he was wrong, and you can't let yourself feel bad for that."

So she was working out her frustrations on this dough and trying not to feel guilty because Scott had done bad things while using her as a justification for it. She still didn't understand why the men in the cartel had taken Bert's daughter though. Cade's face had grown blank when she'd asked.

"I'll explain it when this is over. For now, you just hang out with Grace and I'll let you know what's happening when I can."

She hadn't liked that answer at all, but there was no arguing with her badass Special Operator boyfriend.

Boyfriend? Yeah, she kinda liked that. Though a small part of her thought it wasn't a strong enough word.

"Cade *has* treated me right," she said to Grace as her friend watched her over the marble expanse of the island. "More than right."

"Have you slept with him yet?"

So many emotions in that question. Slept? That was not at all the word to describe what they'd done—multiple times—just last night and this morning. But this was her best friend in the world, and she wasn't going to withhold information. Grace hadn't done that to her once since she'd fallen for Garrett.

"Yes. And it was magnificent," she said, unable to contain the broad smile that broke out over her face.

Grace's eyebrows lifted again. "Wow. I didn't think... You haven't been with anyone that I know of in two years. Have you?"

Brooke felt guilty that she'd kept so much from her friend. She shook her head. "There were things I didn't tell you about that night when I was taken." Grace's face fell, and Brooke rushed over to put an arm around her and squeeze her tight, all while trying not to get flour all over her. "It's okay, sweetie. None of it was your fault, and that's why I never told you. Because I *knew* you would think it was. One of the men—he didn't rape me in the conventional sense, but he put his fingers inside me and threatened me. It's not your fault and it's not Garrett's fault and I'm going to be pissed as hell if you start thinking it is."

"I had no idea," Grace whispered, her voice clearly strained as tears shimmered in her eyes.

"I know. And I still wasn't going to say a word to you about it, but I think—well, I think this thing with Cade has made me realize just how important it is to be honest about everything. It's part of the healing process, and you're my best friend in the whole wide world. I only kept it from you because I knew you'd blame yourself."

Grace caught Brooke's floured hands and squeezed them, uncaring about getting the white stuff all over her pretty clothes. "Yes, of course I would have! Hell, I still feel like you got dragged into that because of me—and I'm so, so sorry."

"I'll tell you like Cade told me—when people choose to do bad things, it doesn't matter if they use you as a justification, it's *not* your fault. You didn't make those choices. They did. Did you know, when your brilliant mind did what it did at the lab, that there were people willing to kill for your research? And that they'd target your friends and family? No, of course not. And once you did know that people would kill for it, you did the best you could to keep it out of enemy hands. Which you were successful at."

"I wish I'd never discovered that damn virus! I've always felt that if there's a global pandemic, it'll somehow be my fault."

"It you hadn't discovered it, someone else would have. And now that the virus is there, you have people working on vaccines. That can't be a bad thing."

Grace sniffed. "Well damn, here I just made this

about me when it's about you and what you went through. I'm sorry he did that to you, Brooke. And that you've been suffering for so long."

"I shouldn't have let it fester. I should have at least told my therapist, which I did not. I know, I know," she said when Grace looked shocked. "I shut it down completely. I thought if I pretended that part didn't happen, then I could deal with it on my own when I learned how to deal with the fear of someone coming in my house and getting me. But I never did." She shrugged. "But Cade told me I needed to tell the doctor. And he's right."

"You told him what happened?"

"Please don't be mad I told him before I told you."

Grace shook her head. "I'm not. I'm just… Wow, I had no idea there was anything between you two. Not like this."

"I hope there's something between us." She bit her lip and glanced at the giant clock on the wall that was part of the French-country decor. "I can't help but worry about him, you know?"

Not that she'd told Grace what was really going on with Scott or Amy Lewis or the cartel. The reason she'd given Grace for coming to stay with her tonight was that Cade had to be at HOT and Brooke didn't want to stay home alone yet.

Grace smiled softly. "I definitely know. Garrett has been gone for over two weeks now. It never gets easier. I think I hoped—no, I *know* I hoped when Daddy got elected that Garrett wouldn't be allowed to go anymore. He fought for the right to stay with his unit though.

How can I try to take that away from him? Or demand he give it up? I can't."

Brooke went back to her dough, rolling it out so she could make biscuits. She didn't know why she wanted to make biscuits, but she found it soothing to play with the dough. Not that she'd offered biscuits in her bakery, but she had offered scones. Similar. Sort of.

"No, you can't. And I guess I can't either. Not that Cade and I are at that stage. But it scares me to think of what he does."

Grace's look was a little sad, a little too knowing. "Yes, it does."

Brooke's stomach was a hard knot cowering in her abdomen. "You never really let on, you know that? I mean I knew, based on my experience with HOT, but I didn't really know. Does that make sense?"

"Perfect sense." Grace stood and came around the island. "Okay, let's stop talking about the bad stuff and get these biscuits in the oven. The girls are coming over, and we've got to get ready."

Brooke's heart skipped. When Grace had told her she was inviting some of the HOT women over for dinner, Brooke hadn't been sure she wanted that. She still wasn't sure. But Grace had already invited them, so there was no backing out now. It wasn't that Brooke didn't know them or like them, but her feelings about Cade were still so raw that she wasn't quite done processing them. How would she hide her fear and worry while they were here?

Her cell phone rang and she jumped on it, flour, lard, and all. It took a couple of tries, in which she smeared her screen with sticky dough, but she got the call answered and held the phone to her ear while her heart pounded.

"Cade?"

"Hi, angel. You doing okay?"

"Fine. You?"

"Doing good. We're still working on this thing. I might not be in touch for a while. Just wanted to let you know that."

Brooke gripped the phone tight, goose bumps prickling her skin. "Okay."

"Gotta go, angel. Think of me tonight."

"I will… Cade?"

"Yeah, angel?"

"I…" She swallowed. "Take care of yourself."

"You too, angel."

The line went dead. Brooke had to remind herself to breathe. Then she turned and pasted on a smile. Grace was frowning.

"Everything okay, Brooke?"

"Yep. Just fine. Let's get busy on the shrimp and grits, okay?"

They worked on the food for another hour, and when it was all hot and piping and perfect, the HOT women showed up. There was Evie Girard, without her kids who were with their nanny; Georgie McKnight; Olivia Blake; Lucky MacDonald; Emily Gordon; Sophie Daniels; Annabelle Davidson; and Christina Marchand. The other women—Gina Hunter, Victoria Brandon, Miranda McCormick, Ivy Erikson, and Kat Mendez— were unable to make it this time.

They crowded around the table, eating and talking for hours. Brooke felt like one of them, though they didn't know she was involved with Cade because she'd asked Grace not to say so just yet. But if and when that happened, she knew she'd love being a part of their sisterhood. They made this life seem so normal, so doable. If they could deal with their men being gone for long stretches, so could she.

By the time the last cupcake was eaten—because of course she'd baked cupcakes after she'd made biscuits—and the last cup of coffee was consumed, it was almost ten o'clock in the evening. They said their goodbyes with hugs and promises to do this again soon.

When the house was empty, Grace yawned and stretched. "Ordinarily I'd suggest we watch a movie together, but I'm beat." She frowned. "In fact, I'm beat quite often these days."

"Pregnancy hormones," Brooke said. "You know that."

"Yes, I do." She sighed. "Still, I guess I'd thought it might be different for me."

"Why? Because you're a hotshot scientist?"

Grace snorted. "Something like that." She stretched, putting a hand on her back as she did. "Good night, Brooke. I love you and I want you to be happy."

"I love you too," Brooke said, hugging her friend. "And I *am* happy."

Grace left her alone in the downstairs. The house was quiet because the Secret Service had their own area and stayed out of the main living quarters. Brooke went and got Max to take him out in the yard for a last run.

A guard nodded to her as she let Max off the leash. She felt safe here, and yet she also felt helpless. Amy Lewis was out there somewhere, scared and alone, and Cade was preparing to head into danger in order to rescue her.

All because Scott had been a criminal asshole who'd fooled Brooke with his bumbling gee-shucks ways.

Her cell phone rang and she glanced at the screen before answering. It wasn't Cade though, but it was still important.

"Bert? Have they found Amy?"

The man on the other end of the line burst into tears. "No, not yet."

Brooke's throat ached. "They will. I know they will. You just have to have faith."

"I'm trying… Miss Sullivan, please, I need your help. It's Shelly…"

Brooke's heart skipped a beat. "What can I do for Shelly?"

"She's losing hope. I need you to talk to her."

"Put her on the line."

"No, please. She needs to see your face, Miss Sullivan. You're the only one she'll believe."

"But I don't know anything…"

"She trusts you. You're honest, and you'll talk her off the ledge. Please." He broke down, and Brooke's throat closed up.

"Where are you?"

"We're at the IHOP." He told her the name of the street. "If you could just come by and talk to her."

Brooke squeezed her eyes shut. Cade had told her

not to leave Grace's house. She didn't want to leave Grace's house.

And yet it wasn't far to the IHOP. She owed poor Shelly Lewis that much, didn't she? She could get a taxi, pop over, and be back in an hour. IHOP was a public place. A taxi wasn't, but so long as the Secret Service put her in it and took down the information, no taxi driver would think of raping her. On the way back— Well, maybe she could get Bert and Shelly to drop her.

"Okay," she said, her throat still tight. "I'll be there in about twenty minutes."

THEY'D BEEN at this for hours now. Cade rubbed his eyes and cracked a yawn. Hacker sat at the computer, the blue light glowing in his face, his concentration not ebbing at all. They'd gone to Brooke's place and retrieved the books. There'd been a flash drive tucked into one of them.

Cade had been angry when they'd discovered it. The motherfucker had put Brooke in danger, not only with his dealings with the cartel but also by using her to hide the evidence. He hadn't been subtle in his obsession, which meant he'd painted a target on Brooke's back too.

Because Bert Lewis knew that Scott was obsessed, and he'd no doubt shared that knowledge with the men who'd paid him for information. Which meant they could reasonably expect that Brooke might have knowledge of where Scott Lloyd had hidden his information.

Cade hadn't told Brooke about Bert. He hadn't been

able to do it, not when she'd been through enough shocks recently. If he'd had to tell her that her favorite security guard was responsible for allowing criminals unauthorized access to the building, it would have crushed her. She had enough to worry about knowing that the cartel had Bert's daughter.

Bert and his wife were currently sitting in a DEA field office, waiting for news about their daughter. Since Bert's involvement in the scheme was murky at best, he wasn't being charged with anything. Yet.

Ivy Erikson was working the case from that side, which meant Viking was here with them, waiting for a go order if the SEALs were needed. He was the liaison between the DEA and HOT at the moment. The whole damned thing was a clusterfuck, and Cade couldn't wait for it to be over.

He wanted to get Amy Lewis to safety, and then he wanted to spend the next couple of days in bed with Brooke.

Hacker was still working on the files. Lloyd had encrypted his information with something a little better than your typical household encryption, and Hacker was busy running his programs, trying to break in.

"Not much longer," he said when he looked up and caught Cade's gaze.

As soon as they had the information on where Lloyd had sent the weapons, they'd have something to negotiate with. At least until they could figure out where Amy was being held so they could go and rescue her.

And then they needed to mop up the cartel's men in the US because if they didn't, Brooke—and Bert, though Cade wasn't too inclined to give a shit about him right now—would never be safe. It pissed Cade off to think of how Lloyd had dragged Brooke back into a world of shadowy players and illegal transactions. The very things she'd never wanted to experience again, and he'd thought nothing of pulling her into his world. Pulling her into danger.

"Halle-fucking-lujah," Hacker said about five minutes later, both fists pumping in the air.

Cade was on his feet. "You got it?"

"I'm in. Need to sort it all out, but the information is — Wow, this shit is detailed. Yeah, I'll find where he stashed ten thousand semi-auto rifles before we're done." Hacker was scanning the documents as he scrolled. "Jesus, this dude was sitting on millions in illegal sales revenue if this is anything to go by."

Cade went to look over his shoulder. Malcolm "Mal" McCoy whistled as he looked over Hacker's other shoulder. "Damn. How many guns did he shuffle for those guys? And how much did he skim for himself without Black Eagle knowing?"

Viking strode into the room with Harley, who'd gone to get him once Hacker broke into the files. The tall blond Navy SEAL looked fierce.

"You've got enough to bury those motherfuckers?"

"Yep, it's all here. It'll take someone with more patience than I have to parse it out, but there's enough here to interest the DEA and ATF for quite some time."

"I'll call Ivy."

Cade glanced up. "Nothing from the Espinozas?"

"Ivy said that Bert got a call, but it wasn't them. It was his supervisor at his regular day job."

"So no more demands then."

"Not yet."

Cade scraped a hand over his head. "I don't like any of this. It's not adding up. They take the little girl, tell Bert to find those files, but then don't call back to demand anything else in hours? Why not?"

"That's a good question," Viking said. "But we won't know anything until he hears from them again." Viking's government-issued phone rang. "Hey, baby."

Cade and the others watched him, wondering if the cartel had made contact with Bert Lewis. But the look on Viking's face wasn't encouraging. In fact, it set the alarm bells in Cade's gut to ringing like they'd been swept up in a tornado.

"Yeah," Viking said grimly. "Thanks, honey. Gotta go. You too."

"What happened?" Cade asked, his gut churning with apprehension.

Viking looked pissed and distressed all at once. "Bert was lying. The call he took wasn't his supervisor at all. It was Andreas Lopez… He made another call after he got off the phone with Lopez. I'm sorry, Saint," he began, and Cade's world started to crack in two. "He called Brooke and told her he needed her help. She left Grace Spencer's house an hour ago. Shit, man, I'm sorry. But they've got her. The cartel took her."

Chapter 20

Brooke was numb. Numb was better than scared, but scared was probably coming. She'd taken a taxi to the IHOP, but when she stepped out of the car, she was grabbed by two men who came out of nowhere. In spite of her screams, she'd been hooded, trussed up like a goose, and tossed onto the floor of a van. All she could think was *it's happening again.*

The men spoke Spanish as they drove, and she listened hard, trying to figure out what they were saying. She didn't know much Spanish, but she knew a little. It was far better to concentrate on that than let herself fall apart. She *refused* to fall apart.

But she didn't know enough Spanish to figure out where they were taking her or who they were. Not that she needed to be told who they were. Certainly they were the Columbians Scott had been selling weapons to. Who else would grab her? Was one of them the man she saw in the hall before she found Scott's body? And what did that mean for her?

She hated to think.

The van screeched to a halt and she was soon yanked out of the vehicle and made to walk while someone gripped her arm like a vise and steered her. The scents of water and fish assaulted her nostrils. She wanted to sink into panic, but she forced herself to focus on what that smell could mean.

The Chesapeake or the Potomac, though she was banking on the Chesapeake. The Potomac wasn't quite this fishy. *Yes, concentrate on details!*

Brooke stumbled along, propelled by cruel hands, until her feet hit a ramp that took her upward. The ramp was hollow—and the structure she stepped onto rolled with the current.

A boat.

A moment later they shoved her into a room where she fell on the floor, her hip hitting a pile of something hard. Brooke's wrists were bound at the front of her body rather than the back, so she reached up to shove the hood off as soon as the door closed.

"Miss Brooke?" a soft little voice asked, and Brooke whipped her head around, searching in the gloomy cabin for the source. As her eyes adjusted, her gaze focused on a little girl in a Girl Scout uniform sitting on the floor.

Brooke gasped as she scrambled toward Amy, gathering her between her bound arms as best she could.

"Amy. Sweetie. How are you?"

"Scared."

Brooke trembled. She'd been holding her own fear at bay behind a giant wall she'd erected, but she knew it was close to tumbling over the top and engulfing her. Except now she needed to keep it together for this little girl. She *had* to keep it together. That's what Cade would do.

The thought of Cade sent a wave of despair—and hope, oddly enough—crashing through her. He would know she was gone by now, wouldn't he? And he'd be angry that she'd left the safety of Grace's house. Grace, with her Secret Service detail and her alarm system complete with cameras and codes and who knew what else?

Things that didn't work so well when you left them behind and ventured out because you wanted to help someone. She couldn't quite reconcile how these men had found her, but they'd probably been watching Grace's place. She should have thought of that and maybe suggested an alternative to Bert. Like what if he'd brought Shelly to her?

She hugged Amy tightly. "It's going to be okay, sweetie. There are some really good men coming to get us soon."

"I don't like the man who brought me here. He wasn't nice."

Brooke's heart skipped. Oh God, if anyone had abused this child… "I know, kiddo. They are *not* nice men at all. But the nice ones are coming."

She had to believe that. Because if she didn't, she'd fall apart—and she was afraid that if she did, she'd never come back together again.

She sat with her arms around Amy and tried to calm her racing heart. She had to keep it together for Amy. And for Cade, because she was determined she would see him again.

"Have you eaten? Did they feed you?" Brooke asked, trying to focus on the most basic things in order to keep from dwelling on the horror of their situation.

"I'm hungry, Miss Brooke." Amy started to cry and Brooke squeezed her tighter.

"I'm sorry, honey. Maybe they'll bring something soon."

She didn't think these bastards intended to bring them anything, but she wasn't going to tell the little girl that.

"Are you okay? Nobody... hurt you, did they? Did they touch you?"

"The bad man picked me up and carried me. Then he put me in here."

Brooke's heart hammered. "Did he do anything else? Did anyone?"

She could feel Amy shake her head. "No." She cried harder. "They left me all alone. I was scared."

"Shh," Brooke said. "It's okay. I'm here now. I won't let them hurt you."

She didn't know how she was going to do it, but she was determined to get Amy out of here without her knowing the sort of terror Brooke had felt at the hands of these kinds of men. Her stomach twisted and she shoved the nausea deep. She couldn't think about that right now. Couldn't worry that it would happen again.

She had to survive for Cade and Max. And she had

to protect this little girl. There was nothing more important.

CADE LOCKED his emotions down and went into crisis mode. He knew his team watched him warily, but he wouldn't blow. Not yet anyway. Not unless something happened and they didn't get Brooke and Amy back again.

It was a good thing Bert Lewis wasn't in this room. Or, hell, this fucking building. Because Cade would likely snap his neck if he saw the man right now. Viking launched into an explanation of how Bert had manipulated Brooke into heading for an IHOP, presumably to comfort his wife, and how Lopez had directed the whole thing. He had *promised* that Amy would be released once the cartel had Brooke. But of course that's not how criminals operated.

No, they operated by being as fucking evil as possible. They'd taken Brooke and they weren't letting her go. It was also entirely possible that the cartel had killed Amy Lewis and dumped her body somewhere.

Ghost strode into the room, looking pissed as shit. Didn't compare to Cade's pissed, but whatever.

"What the fuck is going on over at the DEA?" he demanded of Viking.

Viking didn't look pleased either. "Sir, Bert Lewis was cooperating. He wasn't being held for anything."

Because he was cooperating, the motherfucker. Cade

knew how it worked. And yet he still wanted to strangle the dude.

"Yet they let him use his damned phone. They relied on him to tell them if it was Lopez calling so they could listen in—but he lied when the call came."

"Yes, sir."

"Jesus."

"Yes, sir."

"Have they heard from Lopez again?"

"No, sir."

"What the utter fuck?" Ghost shook his head, hands on hips, looking pissed. Then he spun to Hacker. "What do we have in those files? Do we know where the weapons are yet?"

"No, sir," Hacker said. "Working on it, sir."

"Let me know when you figure it out. And be ready to fucking go when we find them. No way in hell am I leaving this up to anyone else to secure those weapons. HOT is going in."

THEY WERE BEING KEPT in the dirty hold of a fishing boat. Brooke had fallen on ropes earlier. That was the bulky thing she'd hit with her hip. She and Amy had been sitting there for a long time, she wasn't sure how long, when the chattering of voices came to her. She stiffened but kept her hands on Amy. The little girl had stretched out and fallen asleep with her head in Brooke's lap.

Brooke didn't know how long they'd been there, but it felt like a very long time. She was stiff and cold and nauseated from the scents of fish and brackish water. She was also terrified deep down inside, but she'd managed so far to keep it at bay behind a wall she'd erected in her brain. She simply couldn't fail to be the strong one in this situation. Amy was six. She needed a strong adult, not a sobbing woman who couldn't function.

The voices grew closer. They were speaking Spanish. Fear doused her in ice water as the door opened and a light shone in. Brooke blinked, turning her face away and covering Amy's eyes. Two men came over and dragged her and Amy to their feet. Amy started to cry, but Brooke refused to show any emotion.

Though she knew she shouldn't do it, she lifted her chin and faced the men squarely. Neither of them reacted. They simply propelled their charges toward the door and down the ramp. A big black car waited nearby. They were shoved into it unceremoniously and collapsed on the seat in a tangle of bodies.

Brooke's hair fell across her face, covering her vision for a long moment while she worked to sit up and grab hold of Amy before she moved her hair. When she finally managed to shove her hair away, her gaze landed on the man sitting across from her.

The same man she'd seen in the hallway just a couple of nights ago. He arched an eyebrow and smirked at her. There was no warmth in his gaze, however.

"Well, Miss Sullivan. We meet again."

"What do you want with us?"

His gaze flicked to the little girl and then back to her face. Brooke suppressed the shiver that wanted to slide through her at the coldness in his eyes.

"I only want my shipment, Miss Sullivan. Tell me where it is, and you will be free to go."

"Shipment?" She shook her head. "I don't know what you're talking about."

"You were Scott Lloyd's woman."

She shook her head harder. "No. Definitely not. We were friends. That's all."

The man crossed his legs at the knee. He somehow managed to look elegant and polished in spite of the evil in his demeanor.

"That is not how he described it. You were his partner."

Brooke's mouth went dry. "He said that to you?"

The man shrugged. "He implied as much. He said that if anything happened to him, you had the evidence to take down his enemies."

Shock zapped into her neural receptors. "That's not true. I don't know *anything*. We weren't romantic, and I was most definitely not his partner."

"You will understand that I cannot simply take your word for this."

Brooke wanted to ask the man if he'd killed Scott. She knew the answer, but she wanted to hear him say it. And yet she couldn't ask with Amy sitting there and crying. The poor kid was already traumatized.

"I can't tell you anything when I don't know anything. But I can promise you that this child knows absolutely nothing—why don't you let her go? You have me, in spite of the fact that I can't do anything for you."

He laughed. "Ah, Miss Sullivan. I begin to understand why Mr. Lloyd was infatuated with you. Charming. Shrewd. And very beautiful."

Brooke's stomach dropped. Nausea rose in her throat. *No. You control your reaction. You will never be a victim again. Fight.*

"Flattery will get you nowhere, Mister….?"

"Surely you have guessed by now, Miss Sullivan."

"I truly haven't. How could I?"

"Persistent, aren't you?"

"I'm only speaking the truth. I don't know you, I have no idea what Scott was involved in, and hoping I can tell you anything is going to prove fruitless for you."

"Then you can tell me where the files are."

A flush rose on her skin. "Files? What are you talking about?"

He tilted his head to study her. "Ah, finally, something gets a reaction. The files, Miss Sullivan. The ones that your lover deleted off his computer after making a copy. Where is the copy?"

She didn't think that lying about it was going to do her any good at this point. She clearly wasn't good at lying, and he could tell that she knew something. If she continued to insist, then he would never believe her about anything she said.

And maybe he wouldn't anyway, but she wasn't going to lie about something that so obviously made her look guilty. "It might be in a book that Scott returned to me the day he died. But I don't know that for sure, and I don't have the book anymore. The military has it."

"The military? You mean that rather large man you entertained at your apartment the other night?"

"Yes, that's exactly what I mean."

He shook his head. "Well, this is regretful." He pressed a button on the arm of the seat beside him and said something in Spanish. The car started to move, gliding away from the marina.

"Where are we going?" Brooke burst out, her fear getting the better of her.

"Columbia, Miss Sullivan. You had better hope your military man is willing to negotiate—or that you remember some of the information you claim to have forgotten—or you will not enjoy your little trip in the least."

Chapter 21

Six hours later…

"JESUS, is there no end to the sheer amount of contra-band this man was involved in shifting around?" Ghost stood there, looking over Hacker's shoulder, scanning the files that seemed endless.

"It was quite the operation, sir. For someone who only worked at Black Eagle for a little under a year, Lloyd built a network of customers unsurpassed by anything I've seen. He sold a lot of weapons."

"Not an easy thing to do," Ghost grumbled.

Cade paced, his mind on Brooke and what she was very likely going through right now. She had just broken through her fear and managed to share what had happened to her two years ago. Then she'd crossed another barrier when she'd been intimate with him. If anyone touched her this time, he would kill them with his bare hands and deal with the consequences in whatever court he had to. He just prayed that not only did she not suffer abuse but that she also came out of this with her mental health intact.

Though he wasn't sure how that was going to happen. She was still suffering from PTSD over the event two years ago. He hadn't said those words to her, because she'd agreed she needed to go to counseling and that was all he wanted. But now? He truly had no idea what was going to happen to the strides she'd made.

There were other words he hadn't said to her. Important words. Right now it was killing him to think he might never get the chance. Because, damn, he'd fallen for the girl. Hook, line, and sinker. She was unlike anyone he'd ever met. She did things to him that he still didn't understand.

And when he was inside her, rocking into her and hearing her sweet little moans and sighs, there was no other feeling like it in the world. Yeah, he'd fucked his share of women. Had one-night stands, had relationships that went a little longer, relationships that fizzled out after the first hot burst of sexual contact wore off.

But Brooke? No, he wasn't anywhere near done with her. He wasn't sure he ever would be.

He was pissed at her, no doubt about that, because she'd left Grace's house after he'd told her not to, but all he wanted right now was to get her back safe and whole. He'd deal with her inability to follow orders later. After he kissed her a million times or so.

She'd tried to call him, but his phone hadn't been with him because he couldn't bring it into the secure areas of HOT. He'd discovered her message when he'd taken a break and checked it a few hours ago. Hearing her voice had been both painful and breathtaking at once. Painful because it was too late. Breathtaking because it was Brooke.

Now he paced and growled and lashed out from time to time. His teammates kept a wide berth, but they didn't seem to hold it against him.

"Fucking hell," Hacker said excitedly. "I think this is it right here."

Ghost went and stood behind him again. Cade strode to them and peered over Hacker's other shoulder. There were manifests of weapons displayed on the screen.

"Manufacture date," Hacker said, pointing. "Two months ago. Ten thousand, all shipped to... Yes! They're sitting in a container in Panama."

"You're sure those are the guns the cartel wants?" Cade demanded.

"Yep. There's nothing else that matches. Other shipments have been delivered. Others are in the pipeline." He peered a bit closer at the screen. "Looks like there was a dispute over prices. The cartel agreed to one price and then tried to renegotiate when the shipment was delayed. Looks like Lloyd shopped it elsewhere... He had another buyer willing to pay more."

"Holy shit," Cade said. "Dude sold guns to the Espinozas and then sold the guns to someone else? No wonder they killed him."

"Delta Squad is currently in the Central American theater. I'm sending them to seize control of the shipment," Ghost said. "At least we'll have something to negotiate with when Lopez finally gets in touch."

As if on cue, Viking's phone rang. Considering the speed with which he answered, it had to be his wife. A chill slid down Cade's spine. Standing there as if his life wasn't breaking apart while waiting for any news about Brooke was the hardest thing he'd ever done. And he'd done some hard shit over the years.

By the time Viking was finished on the phone, Cade knew it was bad. The SEAL looked grim. "Lopez called Bert again," he said. "He has Brooke and Amy—and they're on the way to Columbia."

Cade's heart dropped. "He's taking them to the Espinoza stronghold."

"Seems so, yes. He has your number, Saint. He wants to deal with you."

Cade didn't have to ask why. If the cartel had been watching Brooke's building, then they'd seen him. And she had his number. He didn't blame her for giving it to them. What choice did she have?

He turned to Hacker. "Can you—"

"On it, boss," Hacker interrupted before he could finish. "Forwarding your calls to the secure line in here."

"Thanks." It wasn't easy trying to separate out duty from love, but he was working on it. He loved Brooke and would do anything it took to get her back. But he had a duty to perform and that came first. Saving her life depended on how he reacted under pressure—and he wasn't reacting unless he absolutely had to. This was not a job for anyone who couldn't shut off the emotions when necessary.

Even if those emotions beat like hell against the lid he'd slammed down on top of them.

Ghost strode from the conference room out onto the command post floor. He left the door open and they could see him go over to coordinate with Major Kennedy, the controller who had responsibility for the teams on the giant map tonight. It was kind of like a game of Battleship, but with dots on a globe instead of ships. The dots weren't trying to sink each other. Rather, they were trying to sink the bad guys wherever they existed.

"Why don't you sit down," Viking said, and Cade blinked. He'd been so intent on Ghost that he hadn't noticed everyone taking a seat.

Cade dragged out a chair and sank into it. It might be hours before Lopez called. Or it might be minutes. And Cade would spend every single moment of it wondering if Brooke was okay or if this was the thing that sent her spinning so hard over the edge that she never came back again.

He prayed it didn't happen that way. That he could get to her and help her before it did.

It was half an hour of hell before the special phone in their secure room rang. Everyone jolted upright. Cade reached for the receiver and then hesitated, exchanging a glance with Hacker, who nodded slowly, verifying that the call was coming from Columbia.

"Hello?" Cade said, though he knew who it was.

Best not to seem like he knew too much though. He didn't want Lopez getting suspicious about what was going on at this end of the conversation. Namely, tracking his ass to a location.

"Ah, Mr. Military Man. It is nice to speak with you."

"Can't say as I feel the same about you, Lopez."

Lopez laughed. "It is going to be like that? Well, never mind. We will get right down to business then. All I want from you is this: my guns. Miss Sullivan says that you have Scott Lloyd's computer files, so you will know where they are by now. Give those to me and you may have Miss Sullivan, as well as Mr. Lewis's delightful little daughter, back again."

Cade burned inside, but he kept the emotion under wraps. "How do I know they're alive and unhurt?"

There was a long pause, and then Brooke's voice came on the line. "Hi, Cade."

The phone was on speaker so everyone could hear it. It killed him that it had to be that way, that everyone would hear her fear and doubt, but it couldn't be helped. A swell of emotion choked him.

"Angel," he said as coolly as he could manage. "Are you okay?"

"Yes. I'm fine. Amy is fine too, though she's scared."

"I'm going to get you out of there, angel. I swear it."

"I know that, Cade. I really do."

Her faith in him rocked him to his core. "Brooke, I—"

"That's enough," Andreas Lopez said. He must have snatched the phone from Brooke and walked away because Cade couldn't hear her at all. His heart thumped and his brain pulsed with fury. "My guns, Cade Rodgers. I want them."

"I don't have them."

Lopez snorted. "Yet. But you will. And when you get them, you will arrange transport to my warehouse in Columbia. If you do not, then I will grind Miss Sullivan and Miss Lewis into little chunks of shark bait. You have two days to make it happen."

"Those guns could be anywhere. How the hell am I supposed to get them to Columbia in two days when I don't even know where they are yet?"

"You will find a way. Or the females will die."

The line went dead. Cade slammed his palm into the table and swore. A hand closed over his shoulder and squeezed.

"We'll get them out," Ghost said. "Hacker, you got a pin on that call yet?"

"I have him. He's in a house in the jungle… Deep in the jungle, near the Brazilian border."

"Good fucking job, soldier. Now let's get to work and start planning our assault."

THEY WERE BEING HELD in a stone house that sat in a clearing surrounded by a dense, wet jungle. The house had shutters from floor to ceiling that opened to let in air, and there were fans whirring overhead. It was hot, oppressively so. Sweat trickled between Brooke's breasts.

She and Amy had been shoved into a small room

with the shutters open and the fans limping along. There was a small bed pushed against one wall, and a bathroom with warm, rusty running water and a stained tub.

Brooke strode to the shutters and stepped out onto the balcony. They were on the second floor, but she could immediately see that escape was not possible. Yes, there were trees that grew right up to the balcony she stood upon, but there was nowhere to go. Plus there were men in dark green fatigues, sweat streaking the fabric beneath their arms and over their chests, who paced back and forth while hugging automatic rifles.

Not the kind of place one escaped from unnoticed. Brooke turned with a growl and headed back inside. Amy lay on the bed, curled into a ball, and quietly sobbed. Brooke went over and sat beside her, rubbing her back as soothingly as possible.

"It'll be okay, honey," she said, though she wasn't sure she believed it. "We'll be okay."

"I want to go home," Amy wailed. "I miss my mommy."

"I know, sweetheart. Soon. I know it will be soon. You'll see your mommy again. Tell me about the last thing you did with her."

Amy sniffed. Brooke wasn't sure her tears were abating, but the kid was thinking and that had to be good.

"We went to see a movie," Amy said. "We had popcorn and hot dogs. It was fun."

"What did you see, honey?"

"*Mary Poppins.*"

Okay, that was not at all the answer Brooke had expected. But there were theaters that sometimes showed old classic movies, which had to be how Amy and Shelly had gone to see it together. Because *Mary Poppins* was ancient. So ancient that Brooke remembered going to see it during a matinee with a friend and her mom. Brooke had fallen asleep. It was all she remembered.

"Did you enjoy it?"

"Yes. Mary flew with an umbrella. And she sang so pretty."

Brooke wished they had that magic umbrella right about now. "What else?"

"There was a man who swept chimneys. He danced and sang."

"What's your favorite movie?"

Amy screwed up her face for a second as she thought about it. "*Frozen.*"

"Why is that?"

"Because Elsa and Anna are brave and strong. Especially Anna. She makes Elsa see that she doesn't have to be afraid."

"Well then, you and I are like Elsa and Anna, right? Because we are brave and strong and we aren't going to be afraid."

Amy smiled, her little tear-streaked face lighting up with hope. "Do you think so?"

Brooke nodded hard. Maybe if she convinced the kid, she'd believe it too. "I absolutely do. We are two princesses trapped by an evil king—but we won't be scared because we're going to win and we're going to get out of here."

"Can I be Elsa?"

"Sure you can."

Amy's face fell. "I wish I had my Elsa costume."

"I wish you did too. But we'll just have to pretend, okay? You are wearing a lovely silver-and-blue gown, and there's a crown on your head."

Amy pretended to straighten the crown. "I should turn those bad men into ice. But my powers aren't working right now."

"They will get what's coming to them, Your Majesty. We just have to be patient. And we mustn't let on that we're royalty when they look at us, okay? That's between us."

"I understand," Amy said, her expression very serious.

The door opened and a woman came inside. She was carrying a tray, and she set it down on a small table before she hurried away again. The scents of meat and onions wafted from the tray. Brooke went over and uncovered the dishes. It wasn't anything fancy, just some soup and bread, but they hadn't eaten in hours now and it was welcome.

Amy came over and stood close by, waiting for Brooke to tell her it was okay to eat. Brooke considered that the food might be drugged but then decided that made little sense when they were already captives. She picked up one bowl and set it near the edge of the table, then did the same with the other. She put the bread between them. There were two bottles of water and they were unopened.

"Let's eat, Your Majesty."

They dragged two chairs over and sat down. Amy

took a careful taste of soup. The kid had manners, that's for sure. Brooke was so hungry she wanted to slurp the stuff up. But she followed Amy's lead and spooned her soup methodically. Even doing that, it didn't take long to eat it all.

They divided the bread and ate all that too. It was basic food but good and filling. Brooke let out a sigh and turned to gaze out the window at the rain that had started to fall. It didn't help the heat. If anything, it made it muggier.

The pat-pat-pat of rain on the leaves was soothing in a way. The scents of earth and flowers permeated the air. Birds called through the trees, and something else chattered from time to time.

"Miss Brooke, there's a monkey!" Amy stood excitedly and ran onto the balcony. Brooke joined her. A gray-and-orange monkey with a long tail and a white face jumped from tree to tree. Another monkey appeared soon after.

Amy laughed. Brooke was glad for that even if it couldn't last. For now they were fed, dry, and they'd been left alone. On the plane, no one had touched either of them. Brooke had started that journey with her stress levels skyrocketing because she'd kept looking at the men on the plane and thinking they were going to abuse her and Amy. She'd even made a plan that if they tried to take her and Amy both, she'd submit voluntarily if they'd leave Amy alone.

But it hadn't happened, and for that she was grateful. She didn't know how she would have gotten through it, but for this child she would have sacrificed herself. Still would if it came down to it.

She desperately hoped it did not because she knew it would break her beyond repair.

The monkeys played and chattered a bit before one of the guards threw something at them. They scampered away, the trees swaying from their passage. Amy stopped laughing and drew in a deep breath. Brooke put her arm around the child and squeezed her shoulder.

"Courage, Elsa."

She could feel the stiffening of the little body beside her. "I'm brave and strong."

"Yes, you are. And so am I," Brooke said. She hoped it was true.

Night fell on the jungle. They curled up on the bed, cocooned within the mosquito netting, and tried to fall asleep. Amy succeeded within minutes. But Brooke lingered, thinking of Cade, thinking of their last moments together and all the things she hadn't said. Hearing his voice on the phone earlier—that had killed her. She'd wanted to tell him she loved him, just in case, but she hadn't wanted to give Lopez that kind of leverage. He already figured they were romantically involved based on the fact Cade had spent the night at her house, but he didn't know more than that.

And she wasn't going to give it to him. Cade was hers alone.

Eventually she dozed to the sound of a million frogs and other creatures singing their arias into the night. It was, in its own way, peaceful. She could almost think she was on a tropical vacation.

But a few hours later an explosion woke her from a dead sleep and shattered all illusions of peace. Brooke's heart crashed into her ribs as a fireball shot into the sky and automatic gunfire sprayed the air.

Someone was coming. But who?

Chapter 22

Cade ran through the jungle clad in a black assault suit, face painted, night vision goggles on, rifle at the ready. It had been a long ride to get here, but they'd HALOed in an hour ago, buried their parachutes and breathing gear, and humped it across the jungle to wind up at the Espinoza Cartel's remote stronghold. Now Echo Squad was executing a precise plan of distracting the cartel's men and infiltrating the facility.

Mal had set off the explosion at the ammo dump a few yards from the main building that housed Andreas Lopez and his drug-smuggling operation. Men ran from their posts to help put out the fire. But there was no putting out the blaze after what Mal had done, even if it was still damp with rain in the air. The explosion had been fantastic, and now the jungle blazed with light that would last a long while.

Cade and Harley, along with teammates Dean "Wolf" Garner and Ryder "Muffin" Hanson, bolted for the house. They'd cut the power to the generators first so that everything would remain dark other than the glow from the fire. They didn't know for certain that Brooke and Amy were in there, but that was the last known location they'd been traced to. Lopez had not called back after he'd hung up on Cade, but Hacker had put a tracer on his phone that indicated he was still here. Every time he called someone, the phone pinged out the location.

Didn't mean he hadn't moved Brooke and Amy, but considering how much trouble it was to get to this location, it wasn't precisely logical to move them when you thought you were impervious to attack.

They weren't though, which Cade thanked his HOT training for. Another group might not try it, but HOT was balls to the wall for this kind of shit. Noah "Easy" Cross and Jax "Gem" Stone had taken up position in a tree nearby and were busy picking off the cartel's men as they ran across open ground.

Cade didn't stop for anything. When he came face-to-face with a cartel member, he shot the asshole and kept on going. The house loomed in front of him now. He put on a last burst of speed and rammed the door open, knocking down a man trying to come through from the other side.

Harley was right behind him, and the two of them ran up the stairs to clear the top floor of the house before heading back down. That's where the bedrooms would be and where it was most likely they'd find Brooke and Amy if they were still here. There was no basement because the ground was too wet, so they already knew not to search for one.

"B team is in," Cade said into the mic on his helmet. "Status reports."

Each two-man team gave a quick report about where they were and what was happening. Dean and Ryder were in the house, clearing the first floor. Cade and Harley kicked in doors on the second floor and swept through rooms. They startled a naked woman who shrieked and dragged the covers up over her body, but they kept going, bursting into rooms, shoving everyone onto the floor and zip-tying their wrists. Naked women included, because you never took it for granted she wasn't involved and dangerous.

But there was no Lopez, and that was worrying. Cade and Harley were a well-oiled team as they moved through the upper level. They kicked in yet another door and burst into the room, weapons at the ready and flashlights shining into eyes in order to blind the targets.

Cade's heart stopped as he processed what was going on. Brooke and Amy sat back to back on two chairs, their bodies bound together with rope, their mouths duct-taped closed. But that wasn't the frightening part. What was frightening was the bomb sitting in Brooke's lap. He could see the wires, the timer, the sticks of dynamite and plastic explosives that held it all together. Her eyes were wide and frightened, but there were no tears.

Andreas Lopez sat in the window, kicking one leg back and forth, a cell phone held in his fingers.

"Ah, so you must be the American military come to rescue these ladies. Noble, gentlemen. Very noble. But I want my guns. If I don't get my guns, I'll press the button on my phone that will send the signal to the detonator."

"You'll blow yourself up too," Cade said.

"Yes, I am aware. But you will have lost this battle because you will blow up with us. I may not have my guns, but the military will not have you—and these women's families will never see them again. So wouldn't it simply be easier to arrange an exchange? Then we all live."

Cade didn't believe that for a moment.

"A cell phone detonator," he said for Hacker's benefit. The IT specialist was listening in from the rendezvous point. Maybe he could disarm it. "Clever."

"Ah yes, that American superiority that thinks we South Americans cannot possibly be as sophisticated. Scott Lloyd thought so too, much to his detriment."

"He tried to sell your guns to someone else."

Lopez perked up. "He did indeed. I take it you found them then."

Cade didn't answer. Lopez shrugged.

"But of course you did, or you would not know this."

Cade could see the rise and fall of Brooke's chest. He kept expecting her or the kid to cry, but neither of them did. All he wanted was to cut the ropes and free them both, take them out of here and figure out the damage somewhere far away where he could give them food and water and a soft bed to lie in.

But they were a long way from those things at the

moment. He had to disarm Lopez first—before the man could blow them all to kingdom come.

"I suggest you take your men and get the hell out of here," Lopez said, dark eyes flashing. "Once you deliver my guns, I'll let these ladies go."

"You won't let them go," Cade said. "You have no intention of doing so."

Lopez smirked. "This is a chance you will have to take, yes?"

"I've blocked his signal, Saint," Hacker growled into Cade's earpiece. "He can't send a flicker of data to the bomb now. But you need to get the phone away from him and cancel any detonation command he's programmed in. With signals being what they are out here, I can't guarantee my jam will hold for more than a couple of minutes."

"Copy that," Cade said. Lopez seemed to think Cade was talking to him, so the dude didn't expect what happened next.

Cade launched himself at Lopez. They fell through the open window and crashed onto the balcony. The phone went skidding across the stone and fell over the side as Cade's heart dropped along with it. *Fuck!*

Lopez aimed an elbow at Cade's windpipe. He barely evaded the maneuver before the man twisted and brought a knee up into Cade's groin.

The blow glanced off the protective gear he wore and Cade growled. "You missed, asshole."

"You need to get that bomb, Saint!" Hacker screamed into his ear. "I'm losing the signal!"

"You can't win," Lopez hissed. "Even if you escape, I will find you. I will find you both, and when I do—"

Cade drew his nine mil and put a bullet through the man's brain.

"Get them out," he shouted at Harley. *"NOW!"*

Cade levered himself up and spun for the door. His leg ached where he'd twisted it during the landing, but he limped through the door and found his teammate cutting the last of the restraints. Cade took the bomb in his hands and went back outside to fling it from the balcony. It left his hands, sailing into the air—and exploded just as Cade made it into the building again. The concussion from the explosion knocked him to his knees. Harley had Brooke and Amy at the other door, pushing them through.

"Go," he yelled, scrambling for purchase as another explosion sounded out in the jungle. More of the ammo blowing. They'd expected that.

"Got a truck," Mal said into the earpiece. "We're wired and ready to go. Everything else is disabled."

"How many bodies?" Cade asked.

"A lot. There'll be a few of them left after this, but not enough to do any damage in the drug world for quite some time."

Cade caught up to his teammate, who was carrying Amy as they flew down the stairs and outside. Brooke ran beside him, head down and determined. Her mouth wasn't taped anymore. He knew that Harley hadn't removed the tape because there'd been no time. Which meant Brooke had done it herself. Ripped duct tape off her mouth, which he knew from experience hurt like a motherfucker.

They hurtled toward the truck that Mal was sitting in, all of Echo Squad converging at once. Except for the two snipers, who would join them when they passed by their hideout in the tree. Harley handed Amy to someone in the truck and then reached for Brooke. She shrank away, but Cade was there, gripping her shoulders firmly. Harley jumped inside and let Cade handle it.

"Need to get you inside," he said in her ear.

She nodded and he helped her into the truck where she took a seat beside Amy. Cade clambered in and flopped onto the seat. The rest of the team piled inside. When they were all there, Mal pressed the gas and the truck shot down the dirt road toward the trees. A quick pause for Noah and Jax to drop into the vehicle, and Echo Squad was barreling down the road as the Espinoza Cartel's ammo dump turned the sky orange behind them.

Cade wanted to drag Brooke into his arms, but Amy was between them. Instead, he put a hand on the nape of her neck. She turned her gaze to him. He held his breath for a long minute, wondering what he would see. But then she smiled. And his world got knocked sideways by the beauty in that smile.

Brooke was his. And he planned to tell her about it just as soon as he got a chance.

BROOKE THOUGHT they probably drove for a couple

of hours, though she dozed a bit here and there, until they reached a site where a military helicopter was waiting, the rotors beating the air into a tornado around them. Brooke kept Amy in her sights, though the men took good care of her, carrying her from truck to helicopter, belting her in, telling her not to be afraid.

But Amy wasn't afraid, not anymore. She'd been in character now for a while, and Brooke was so darn proud of the kid she could burst. But she was also worried because what if pretending to be someone else in order to stay strong was a mistake? What if Amy had long-term problems from this?

What if she ended up like Brooke, afraid of her own shadow and unable to form normal relationships with people? And what if that was Brooke's fault for suggesting they pretend to be Elsa and Anna in the first place?

Brooke brooded on these thoughts during the flight. She was across from Cade rather than next to him like she wanted to be. When he'd burst through that door earlier, she'd been so relieved and happy. And scared, of course, because Lopez was crazy enough to detonate the bomb if provoked.

When Cade had launched himself at Lopez, her heart lodged in her throat and her life flashed before her eyes. But then there was the sound of a gunshot and Cade was back, apparently unhurt, to grab the bomb from her lap and throw it. Every moment of that maneuver was etched into her mind, from the hard look on his face to the way he didn't hesitate to pick up a live bomb and carry it away from her.

She'd been avoiding the thought of the gunshot as much as she could, but there was no avoiding it any longer. Cade had tackled Lopez and they'd fallen out the open window. Cade came back and Lopez did not, which meant that Lopez was the one who'd been shot. He hadn't shot himself. And since he hadn't come back at all, Cade had clearly killed him.

She examined her feelings about that. There was horror and fear—and there was relief too. Cade had killed the man who'd killed Scott and planned to kill her and Amy. He'd threatened to turn them into shark bait. He'd strapped a bomb to them. He did not care about their lives, so she wasn't going to care about his. He'd made his choice, and he'd paid a price for it.

The helicopter soon landed on a military base. Everyone transferred to a plane that sat with engines running. They wasted no time in taking off. Once they were in the air and the plane had passed the ten-thousand-foot threshold, Cade unbuckled her seat belt, lifted the arm between them, and dragged her into his embrace. He didn't kiss her. He merely put his face into her hair and breathed her in.

He smelled like smoke and sweat and grease. She didn't care. She wrapped her arms around him and pressed her cheek to his, uncaring if she got his dark greasepaint on her.

"I love you," he whispered in her ear.

Brooke stilled. She wasn't certain she'd heard him right at first. She didn't say anything for a long moment, breathing, trying to recall the words he'd said in precisely the order he'd said them. Had he really just said…?

"I should have told you before. I should have let you know how I feel."

She pushed back so she could see his face. He was covered in greasepaint and sweat and she thought she'd never seen anything so wonderful in her life. When he'd fallen out that window with Lopez— Well, she'd nearly sucked the duct tape down her throat with the gasp she'd attempted to utter. And then the gunshot, which had made the world stand still until she'd heard his voice. She had to face that this was his life—chaotic, dangerous, messy, and violent. And it wasn't going to change. Could she handle it?

"I love you too," she said in a rush before she could think too hard. "Madly. And I know I shouldn't have left Grace's house. I just thought— Well, I felt guilty that Amy had been kidnapped and I wanted to help. Bert was so distraught, and Shelly—" She swallowed. "Amy's their only child. I thought I could help."

Cade looked troubled. She knew he was probably angry with her for not listening to his instructions, which was why she'd felt she had to apologize.

"It's my fault," he said. "I should have told you the truth."

"Truth?"

He glanced over at Amy, who was playing with an iPad someone had given her. Watching *Frozen*, it appeared.

Cade pitched his voice low. "Bert let Lopez into the building. He also erased the security recordings where

Lopez appeared. And he set you up so Lopez could grab you at the IHOP."

Shock washed over her. Bert? Her friend? He'd betrayed her? "But why? Why would he do that?"

"His wife has multiple sclerosis. He needed the money that Lloyd and the cartel paid him to keep their meetings with Scott Lloyd secret. And then he needed to do what Lopez told him or he might end up dead as well."

Brooke was stunned. "Shelly has MS?"

"Yes."

"Oh, poor Bert."

He frowned. "That's your reaction to him setting you up? Poor Bert?"

"No, it's not my whole reaction. I'll get mad soon enough. But right now—well, I can't imagine what he must be going through."

"He put his family in danger. And you too. I'm not so inclined to think poor Bert right now."

Brooke glanced at Amy. "She's safe. So am I. And Bert's going to suffer for this because he put his child in danger. She'll have nightmares. She'll need therapy. He's not going to ever forget what he did to her."

Cade brushed her hair back from her face, his fingers gentle against her cheek. "What about you, angel? How are you really? Because I'm worried."

She thought about it. Really thought about it. Everything that had happened over the past twenty-four hours. And though it scared her, as it should, she didn't feel that throat-closing panic she'd gotten before.

"I think I'm okay. I mean I'm not going to magically

process this and act like nothing ever happened, but I think I know what I need to do this time. I need to talk to my counselor. And no, nothing happened to me this time. No sexual assaults at all. And they didn't touch Amy either. They scared us, but I think Lopez must have issued orders about leaving us alone—or they just weren't interested. Not one man copped a feel. Not one."

"You're brave, you know that?"

She smiled. "Actually, I do. Brave and strong. Amy and I pretended to be Elsa and Anna from *Frozen*. I did it to help Amy—but I think it may have helped me too. I had to stay strong for her. And I did."

His gaze searched her face. He put a finger on her mouth, skimmed it over her lips. "You ripped the tape off."

"I didn't rip it. I pulled steadily. No worse than hot wax."

He snickered. "You crack me up sometimes, angel."

"Do you want to kiss me, Cade?"

His gaze dropped to her lips. "I definitely do. I'm a little worried about the tenderness though."

"Then I'll kiss you."

Chapter 23

It took far too long for the plane to reach DC, and then it took even longer for the mission debriefing and medical checkups that were a necessary part of operations. Brooke and Amy were taken to a private medical facility that usually evaluated the people HOT brought back. It was an exclusive place, accustomed to the kinds of injuries and psychological issues that hostages could have. Cade was glad that Brooke was being seen there, but she'd been seen there before and she'd still managed to hide the things that had happened to her from the medical professionals on duty.

She'd sworn she was okay this time, and he believed her. But still he worried.

When she'd touched her mouth to his on the plane, he'd groaned and hugged her close. The guys very wisely didn't comment, though once they were on the ground and Brooke and Amy were taken by ambulance to the medical facility, he'd taken some ribbing.

"Cade and Brooke, sitting in a tree, *k-i-s-s-i-n-g...*," Mal said. The others took up the ditty and teased him all the way back to HOT HQ. Except for Hacker, he'd noticed. Hacker didn't say a word.

"Laugh it up, assholes," Cade had said. "But your day is coming. *If* you're lucky."

"Not me," Mal declared. The others followed suit. Hacker had turned away and gazed out the window. Cade figured he was just tired. Hell, they were all tired.

Now Cade stood in the shower and let the hot water hit aching muscles. His hip and leg hurt where he'd landed on them when tackling Lopez. There'd be bruising, and he had muscle relaxers if he needed them.

But he didn't care about his aches and pains so much as he cared about Brooke's. He was dying to get to her, especially after what they'd said to each other on the plane, but he had to wait. She'd promised to call him when she was done. Her cell phone was gone since Lopez had confiscated it when she'd been taken, but she swore she had his number memorized and she would use a phone at the hospital and call him.

He finished showering, got dressed, and headed for his truck. His phone buzzed in his pocket and he stopped to fish it out and look at it.

Brooke: *Hey, handsome. How are you?*

His heart throbbed. *I'm good. How about you? Where are you? And how did you get a phone?*

Brooke: *Grace. She got me a new phone. She was waiting for me when I finished. Insisted on bringing me back to her place. Garrett is home.*

Oh hell, he hadn't even realized Alpha Squad was

back. He'd been so preoccupied with this mission, and with Brooke, that he hadn't paid attention.

I want to see you, angel. NOW.

Brooke: *And I want to see you, Cade. Come and get me and Max. I need to see you and hold you and get your* [eggplant] *in my* [cat] *as soon as possible.*

Cade snorted a laugh. Was she really okay? Could it be that easy? Guilt followed hard on the heels of his happiness. He'd told her he loved her. She'd told him she loved him. But he was still who he was, and she was a woman who didn't like the kind of life he led.

I'm coming.

Brooke: [waggling eyebrow emoji] *You will be.*

I love you, angel. Crazy love. You know that, right?

She sent back a string of hearts. *Yes! I love you too. Which is why I want your* [eggplant].

He didn't think it was as easy as that—they were going to have to talk first—but he hopped in his truck and fired it up. He wasn't sure what was going to be the hardest—talking with Brooke about what had happened and where they were going or getting through Iceman and Grace and convincing them he was in love with Brooke Sullivan.

For better or worse.

BROOKE WAS NERVOUS, and not just because Grace was overly chipper and Garrett looked grumpy. They talked to her like she was made of eggshells, speaking to her like a light breeze would blow her over and she'd shatter. It was annoying.

Cade didn't talk to her that way. In fact, Cade treated her like she was made of stronger stuff, though he also made sure she was holding up when things got tough. But he gave her the benefit of the doubt, and she appreciated that.

Still, she knew her friends were coming from a place of love and she couldn't be mad at them for it even if she wanted to scream sometimes.

Max was his usual self, happy to see her, licking and whining and jumping up and down when she walked in the door. She hadn't wanted to go to Grace and Garrett's other than to get Max, but of course they'd known what was happening and they'd also known the instant she'd returned. Since Garrett was HOT, he knew where to find her.

They'd been waiting for her when she'd been released from her evaluation. She'd been dehydrated and exhausted but otherwise healthy. She'd demanded information on Amy and been assured that the little girl was well and her parents were with her. Brooke hadn't wanted to see Bert, so when she'd emerged to find Garrett and Grace waiting, she'd gone with them with very little argument.

They'd stopped so she could get a new phone on the way. Since all her contacts were in the cloud, she'd been able to restore her phone and access her conversations with Cade. She didn't tell her friends that she'd texted Cade because she didn't want to hear any arguments against it.

When his truck pulled up a short while later, she knew he'd have to be buzzed into the house by the Secret Service. She'd gotten out easily enough two nights ago because she wasn't their charge and they weren't assigned to her. But getting in when you weren't expected would be a whole other story.

A few minutes passed and no Cade, so Brooke returned to the window to see what was happening—and there were Garrett and Cade, facing each other with fists clenched and red faces. The Secret Service guys didn't even bother to interfere. They knew better.

Brooke bolted down the hall, ripped open the side entry door and bounded outside to where the men stood.

"What are you doing?" she shouted.

Garrett spun. "Get back inside, Brooke." He was calm and almost fatherly with her. She wanted to smack him. And kiss him on the cheek for being so sweetly irritating. She knew he still felt guilty for what had happened to her, just as Grace did. That's why they were so protective. Her family was in California, so Garrett and Grace felt responsible for her. She loved them for that, but it was also suffocating.

"No, Garrett. Let Cade in. I want him here. We can talk like adults inside."

Garrett frowned. And then he let out a breath. "Fine. Let's go."

They went back inside, and Brooke led the way to the TV room where so many football games had happened. Where these men had been friends and had a good time together.

Grace appeared, having gone to take a nap when they'd returned home earlier. She looked refreshed, though she also looked puzzled.

"Oh. Hello, Cade," she said when she realized he was there too.

"Hi, Grace."

Brooke marched to his side and twined her fingers in his. Garrett looked to Grace with a huge frown but didn't say anything. Grace sighed.

"Look, I love you two," Brooke said. "And I know you're only looking out for me. You care about me and you care what happens to me. I wasn't truthful with you about what happened two years ago." She knew Grace would have told Garrett by now. A muscle in his jaw tensed and she knew it was true. "But I'm going to be fine. And I'm going to be fine because of this man right here."

Cade squeezed her fingers. "I understand that you two are worried about Brooke," he said. "But you have nothing to fear from me. I love her. I intend to marry her whenever she's ready. And if she's not ready for ten years, well, I'll marry her then."

Butterflies beat in her belly. "You want to marry me?"

"When you're ready."

"You don't even know if I have any disgusting habits yet—what if I clip my toenails at the breakfast table? Or wear the same socks for a week?"

He grinned. "Then I'll make sure we don't sit at the table for breakfast, and I'll wash your dirty clothes every day."

Grace still looked dubious. Garrett looked thought-ful. Brooke let go of Cade and went over to her bestie. She had to stand on tiptoe to kiss her friend's cheek. Then she took both of Grace's hands and held them in hers. "You're emotional right now. Your hormones are going crazy and you love me. But honey, *you* fell for Garrett in a matter of days. And he fell for you. Now tell me that your hasty romance has ruined your life or that you're miserable with this man and looking for a way out. Tell me it isn't working out and you made a mistake. Tell me that, and I'll tell Cade to go away and I won't see him again."

Grace only blinked, her mouth falling slightly open. Garrett was actually grinning when Brooke shot him a glance. He came over and put his arm around Grace, pulled her into his side, and kissed the top of her head.

"Admit it, cupcake," he said. "You've been outma-neuvered. She's right."

Grace let out a long breath. "You're right. We already talked about it, I know, but I wondered if maybe you weren't infatuated. And I wondered if Cade was really capable of giving you what you deserve." Her gaze lifted, went to Cade standing nearby. "I think he is, by the way. He's almost as romantic as Garrett."

Garrett snorted. "Cupcake, he's *way more* romantic than I am. I'm not romantic at all. I just knew you were the one for me and I was going to do whatever it took to let you know. Saint here—well, he seems about as likely to spout poetry as my great-aunt Mary. Which, as you know, happens often and tends to be flowery as shit."

Brooke stifled a giggle. She'd heard all about Great-aunt Mary. She spoke in Shakespearean sonnets when particularly moved, and she could quote Emily Dickinson and Wordsworth all day long. Grace laughed about the way the woman would launch into sonnets at the Olive Garden whenever they went back to visit Garrett's family. Apparently the breadsticks there were worthy of great poetry.

"Hey, I don't spout poetry," Cade protested. "I mean, I'll learn if she wants it, but hell, dude, when have you ever heard me say anything poetic?"

Grace laughed suddenly and hugged Brooke. "Congratulations, bestie. I mean it. Clearly if Saint can put up with us, he really does have the patience of a saint. And he deserves you."

Garrett shook Cade's hand. "Just kidding with you, man," Garrett said. "You aren't bright enough to memorize a poem."

"Gee, thanks," Cade replied.

"Okay, so I'm not her dad or anything—and understand she's still got one of those you'll have to go through. A fancy doctor out there in California or something, so good luck with that—but I'm obliged to tell you, on behalf of my wife, that if you hurt Brooke or break her heart, I'll have to beat your ass into a pulp."

"Roger that," Cade said.

"Okay, great," Garrett replied, stepping back with arms wide. "Can we fucking get something to eat now? I'm starving."

Chapter 24

He had every intention of taking it slow with her after her ordeal, but Brooke had other ideas. Ideas that shocked Cade considering that he'd figured she'd just want to cuddle up in his arms and sleep.

He took her to his place so they could let Max out to run if he wanted, and because it was closer, and no sooner were they inside than he had her in his arms. He intended to hold her close, just hold her, but Brooke had her hands beneath his T-shirt, her palms on his skin, searing into him, within seconds.

She stood on tiptoe, sought his mouth. He obliged her—because he'd be crazy not to—taking her mouth in a hot, wet kiss that curled toes. His cock was stone in his pants.

"Brooke, baby, angel—we don't have to do this tonight," he said. "We've got forever. You can sleep and I'll take care of you."

She pushed back, her baby blues gazing up at him

with such heat and need that his heart did a somersault. *Daaaamn…*

"I love you, Cade. You love me. I almost didn't get to tell you that, and I almost didn't get to be with you again. I want you so desperately I hurt. I want you inside me. I want your cock and your tongue, and I want your arms around me. I want to be together in the closest way possible. *I need it.*"

That was all he needed to hear. Cade went to work doing one of the things he did best. He took total control, willing to give it back if she needed it, but she didn't. He stripped her naked, dropped to his knees, and licked her pussy until she cried out, shuddering hard as she came on his tongue.

Then he picked her up and took her to the bedroom. Within seconds, he was naked and inside her, thrusting deeply into her body.

"Tell me if it's too much," he said.

Her fingers dug into his back. "Not enough," she said. "Never enough with you."

He knew exactly what she meant. He fused his mouth to hers and pumped into her harder, taking them both higher and higher. But before he could explode, he rolled with her until she was on top.

Brooke squeaked at the change in position. He held her hips, gazing up at all that hot blond beauty, those lusciously large tits, her narrow waist and wide hips. This woman was built like a wet dream. His wet dream.

"Ride me, angel," he told her. "I want to watch you come."

Her hands pressed into his chest, holding her body

up as she began to move, rising and sinking on his cock over and over. He made a mental note to get a big standing mirror that he could position to watch them fuck in every conceivable position he could think of.

"That's it, Brooke," he said as her tits swayed and she bit her lip and moaned.

For good measure, he put his fingers between them and strummed her clit.

"Oh my God," she gasped. "I'm going to come..."

He was too. It hit him like a vise to the balls, though a pleasurable one that squeezed everything together before opening the flood gates. As he poured himself into her, he groaned and lifted his head so he could suck one of her sweet nipples deep while his body shook and spent itself in a hot rush.

Slowly she collapsed on him, her skin moist with sweat, the scent of her surrounding him. She rested a palm on his chest. The other hand was a little higher, on his shoulder.

He skimmed the pads of his fingers down her spine, over her ass. His throat tightened for a moment. This woman loved him. Trusted him. After everything she'd been through two years ago—and everything now—she trusted him enough to let herself go like this.

It humbled him. He would never take that trust for granted.

"I love you," she said against his chest. "I needed that so much."

"I love you too. And I'm glad you needed it. I too, but I didn't want to push you."

She lifted her head to gaze at him. Her

soft. "You made me whole again, Cade. I know I still have to talk to my therapist, and I will, but you showed me that I *am* strong and I *am* capable of living my life without constant and debilitating fear. I'm not miraculously cured—but I love you and trust you and it's easy to let myself go with you."

He knew what a gift that was. How hard it had to have been for her to make that leap.

"I'll always protect you, angel." But he'd also been thinking, and he needed to say it. "But if you decide this isn't for you, that you can't handle my life, I'll understand. I'll let you go, though it'll kill me to do it. I don't ever want to drag you into something you don't want. I don't want you worrying about the danger or about it carrying over to you ever again."

She frowned. "Do you honestly think my love is that weak? That I'm going to walk away because life is scary and your life is scarier than most?" She shook her head and her hair flew around her face. "No way, Jose. I'm addicted to your eggplant. I'm addicted to *you*. Am I going to get scared? Yep. Am I going to huddle up with Grace and her kid and be terrified because you're incommunicado? Yes. But what kind of idiot would I be if I took all this"—she waved a hand up and down their bodies—"and threw it away? Not happening."

"Amazingly enough, you're making me hard again."

"Like you ever stopped? You're still inside me, and nothing has changed."

He flipped her over and spread her wide. "Then hold on, angel. I'm about to rock your world."

"Again?" she asked, one eyebrow arched. "Bring it on, my love. I am *so* ready."

THE SUN WAS STREAMING into the room when Brooke woke and stretched. Her body was sore, some of it due to her captivity, some of it due to Cade. The parts that were due to Cade made her shiver in delight.

They'd made love more times last night than she'd have thought possible. They'd sleep and wake and fuck, and then sleep and wake and fuck some more. It was amazing and beautiful and addictive. No wonder Grace was so happy all the time and had been since Garrett had saved her. They couldn't keep their hands off each other, and Brooke finally understood what that felt like.

Even with Gavin, the man she'd thought she'd loved before she found out he had a wife, she'd never had this constant need to touch and get naked that she had with Cade.

"Morning, angel," Cade said. She pushed herself up on an elbow and watched as he carried a tray into the room. He was wearing his tighty-whities, his entire body simply the most beautiful thing she'd ever seen with its ridges of honed muscle and its long, perfect lines. If she were an artist, she'd sculpt him.

"Morning," she said as happiness suffused her. "Did you fix breakfast?"

"Yep. Eggs, bacon, toast. And coffee of course. Sound good?"

"Definitely." She sat up and he put the tray down on

the bed, joining her under the covers and scooting the tray up so they could share the plates. And he'd literally piled eggs and bacon and toast on one big plate. There were two forks and two cups of coffee.

"I can get you a plate of your own if you want. It was easier to carry this way."

She stabbed her fork into the eggs. "This is fine. I love sharing with you."

"Max has been fed, and he went out to chase squirrels in the yard."

Brooke laughed. "He's going to get so spoiled running around out there."

"Look, I know it's too soon to talk about these things, but if you want to stay with me for a while, you and Max are welcome. I'm happy to come stay with you too. Not that we're moving in together, but when we do, I'm happy to do what makes you happy."

"You are the perfect man, Cade Rodgers with a *D*. Hot sex, hot breakfast, and you took care of my dog. I'd be crazy not to spend as much time with you as I can."

He bit off a piece of bacon and grinned. "You would."

"I like it here. My job is portable, and quite honestly I don't think I want to live in my condo anymore. Bad memories there. So maybe I can stay here with you while I work to put my place on the market. After that, we can talk about the next step."

"Sounds reasonable to me," he said. "But angel, you need to know something." His gaze was serious, his gray eyes beautiful and sigh-worthy as he laid all his considerable charm on her. "I'm taking it easy for you, but I'm all in. I've been feeling lost for the past few years now, my relationships empty and unfulfilling. I'm tired of sex without commitment and tired of not having someone to plan a future with. You're my someone, angel. Just so you know, the next step for me will always involve you."

Her heart was a warm puddle of joy. Her throat was tight. "I'm so glad I texted you that day. I hate to think that none of this would have happened if I hadn't."

"It was happening, angel."

She blinked. "You can't be sure of that."

"Yeah, I can. Because it was meant to be. And meant to be always finds a way."

"I love you."

"You do. Because you were meant to. And I was meant to love you." He shrugged and fed her a forkful of eggs. "Karma, kismet, destiny. I don't care what you call it. It's real. You in my bed is proof of it."

"Marriage, huh?" she asked when she'd swallowed the eggs. "Kids too?"

"If you want them."

"Do you?"

He reached out and skimmed a finger over her cheek, tucking her hair behind her ear. "I think a little girl who looks like her mommy would be amazing."

"Or a little boy who looks like his hot daddy?"

"That too. Or none at all, if that's what you want. Or if it's the card life deals us. Not every couple can have babies."

"You'd be okay with that?"

"So long as I have you, yes. Besides, there's always adoption if we wanted to try another way."

"That's true. Wow, this is sounding like a serious plan."

"It is."

She leaned over and kissed him. He tasted like bacon and coffee. "You know what I think?"

"What?"

"I think life with you is going to be amazing. And I can't wait to get started."

He threaded his fingers into her hair, kissed her lazily and long. "It already is amazing, angel. I'm a lucky man—and I plan to show my appreciation every single day."

"Mmm, I love that plan…"

"I knew you would. Now finish your breakfast so I can have dessert."

She didn't have to ask what he was talking about. The twinkle in his eyes told her exactly what he was planning to do.

Lucky girl…

Yes, she was.

Chapter 25

One month later...

SKY KELLEY NURSED his beer and let his gaze swing over the gathering at Garrett Spencer's house. It was another football Sunday, and the guys from Alpha, Echo, and the SEALs were all there. The ones who'd paired up had their women with them, though the women were currently in the kitchen discussing Grace Spencer's impending baby.

Saint ambled by with a fresh beer, then backed up and flopped down beside Sky.

"You okay, Hack?" he asked, frowning.

Sky didn't bat an eye. "Sure. Why are you asking?"

"You've been quiet lately. Quieter than usual, I mean."

"Nothing much. Thinking."

"Yeah, guess you got a lot to think about."

Sky frowned. What did that mean?

"With the computer stuff and all," Saint continued. "Don't know how you do it, but glad you do."

Sky shrugged. *Familiar ground.* "We all have our gifts. Understanding how systems work is mine."

"Yeah, well, if you hadn't jammed that signal out there in the Columbian jungle…" He shuddered, frowning.

"You've thanked me enough, Saint. It's what we do, right?"

"Yeah." He sucked in a breath and leaned his head back on the chair he'd sat down in.

"How's she been?" Sky asked.

Brooke Sullivan seemed to have recovered from the ordeal just fine, but you could never tell if there was any lingering damage. Not to mention it hadn't been the first time she'd been involved on the wrong end of a mission.

"She's doing great. Occasional nightmare, but nothing lasting. Just accepted an offer on her condo a couple of days ago. We're moving to a new place, and Brooke is opening up a bakery."

"Oh man, those donuts you brought into work last week…"

"Yeah, right? Girl can whip up sweets that'll make a grown man beg."

Sky snorted. "You don't say?"

"Mind out of the gutter. That's my lady."

Sky clinked his beer bottle with Saint's. "I know. Just teasing. How's the Lewis kid, by the way?"

Saint frowned. "She's good, actually. Making progress. Brooke sees her a couple of times a week."

"And Bert Lewis?"

"They've spoken once. He's apologetic as hell, but I don't think she's going to forgive him anytime soon. Neither will his wife, it seems. He lost his job, he's under indictment for conspiracy, and his wife left him. Not that he was actually involved in the cartel's gunrunning, but he covered for their meetings with Scott Lloyd—and erased the footage that proved Lopez was the one who'd pulled the trigger."

"Guess he should have thought of what might happen before he got involved with the Espinozas. Though trying to take care of his wife... Well, it's understandable in a way."

Saint didn't look convinced. "There has to be other ways. He fucked up, and he nearly got Brooke and his daughter killed in the process."

"True," Sky said.

"At least they're out of business for a while."

The Espinoza Cartel was suffering from the attack on their stronghold and from the loss of the weapons they'd paid for and never gotten. But they'd be back to strength in a year or so. Maybe sooner.

The information in Scott Lloyd's digital files had taken down Black Eagle Firearms once and for all. The top-tier management had been indicted, and a few of them were busy trying to make plea deals. Motherfuckers, all of them.

Brooke came sashaying back into the living room, and Saint pulled her down on his lap and nuzzled her neck. She giggled and they shared a few private words that Sky could tell were intense.

He turned away and chugged his beer. Then he stood and they looked up at him, happy faces striking a deep chord within him. A melancholy chord.

What the fuck?

"Got an appointment in the morning," he said. "So I'm going to get out of here."

"You got a ride?" Saint asked.

"I Ubered over."

Saint nodded. "See you later."

Sky took his leave of the party, dialed an Uber, and headed for the small town house he was renting near the military post. When he got inside, he grabbed another beer from the fridge, then flopped onto the couch and opened his laptop.

The email he hadn't clicked for days was still there. Still staring at him. He stared back, drinking beer and telling himself there was no way in hell he was going to open it. She wouldn't know if he read it, but *he* would know.

And he didn't want her in his headspace. Not again. She'd done enough damage.

Sky minimized the email, as he had every day since it arrived, and went searching in some of the forums he frequented, seeing what was going on in the world and who was making news. He finished the beer and opened another one.

The email window was still there though, still bugging him. He maximized the window again. And then he clicked the email before he could change his mind. It was going to eat him alive if he didn't—hell, it had already started.

He stared at the blinking cursor. And then, like ripping off a bandage, he decided to just get it over with. To click the fucker and find out what she could possibly have to say after all this time.

The message opened, taking up his screen. The words seared into his eyeballs.

Sky, I need to see you. Please. Bliss

SKY SNAPPED the laptop closed with a growl. He got up, intending to get another beer—and then another and another. Time to get knee-walking drunk.

The doorbell rang. He went over and looked out the peephole, expecting it was Mrs. Ernst wanting a cup of sugar or something. She found an excuse to visit him about once every couple of days. He was used to it by now, even if he wasn't really prepared to deal with her.

But it wasn't Mrs. Ernst. His heart stopped in his chest as he stared at the small figure on the other side of the door. Sleek dark hair, full lips, wide-set eyes, an air of innocence that was an absolute fucking lie.

He felt nothing at seeing that face. Nothing at all.

And then he felt everything. Anger, hot and swift, flooded him. He jerked the door open before he could think better of it.

She smiled tentatively. "Hello, Sky. It's been a while."

Rage urged him to slam the door. Curiosity wouldn't let him.

"What the hell do you want, Bliss?"

She arched an eyebrow and wrapped a mantle of self-righteousness around her shoulders. "Is that any way to talk to your wife?"

Who's HOT?

Alpha Squad
Matt "Richie Rich" Girard (Book 0 & 1)
Sam "Knight Rider" McKnight (Book 2)
Billy "the Kid" Blake (Book 3)
Kev "Big Mac" MacDonald (Book 4)
Jack "Hawk" Hunter (Book 5)
Nick "Brandy" Brandon (Book 6)
Garrett "Iceman" Spencer (Book 7)
Ryan "Flash" Gordon (Book 8)
Chase "Fiddler" Daniels (Book 9)
Dex "Double Dee" Davidson (Book 10)

Commander
John "Viper" Mendez (Book 11)

Deputy Commander
Alex "Ghost" Bishop

Echo Squad

Cade "Saint" Rodgers (Book 12)
Sky "Hacker" Kelley (Book 13)
Malcom "Mal" McCoy
Jake "Harley" Ryan (HOT WITNESS)
Jax "Gem" Stone
Noah "Easy" Cross
Ryder "Muffin" Hanson
Dean "Wolf" Garner

SEAL Team

Dane "Viking" Erikson (Book 1)
Remy "Cage" Marchand (Book 2)
Cody "Cowboy" McCormick (Book 3)
Cash "Money" McQuaid (Book 4 - Coming soon!)
Alex "Camel" Kamarov
Adam "Blade" Garrison
Ryan "Dirty Harry" Callahan
Zach "Neo" Anderson

Black's Bandits

Ian Black
Brett Wheeler
Rascal
? Unnamed Team Members

Freelance Contractors

Lucinda "Lucky" San Ramos, now MacDonald (Book 4)
Victoria "Vee" Royal, now Brandon (Book 6)
Emily Royal, now Gordon (Book 8)

Also by Lynn Raye Harris

The Hostile Operations Team Books

Book 11: HOT VALOR - Mendez & Kat

Book 12: HOT ANGEL - Cade & Brooke

The HOT SEAL Team Books

Book 1: HOT SEAL - Dane & Ivy

Book 2: HOT SEAL Lover - Remy & Christina

Book 3: HOT SEAL Rescue - Cody & Miranda

Book 4: HOT SEAL BRIDE - Cash & Ella

Book 5: HOT SEAL REDEMPTION - Alex & Bailey

The HOT Novella in Liliana Hart's MacKenzie Family Series

HOT WITNESS - Jake & Eva

About the Author

Lynn Raye Harris is the *New York Times* and *USA Today* bestselling author of the HOSTILE OPERATIONS TEAM SERIES of military romances as well as twenty books for Harlequin Presents. A former finalist for the Romance Writers of America's Golden Heart Award and the National Readers Choice Award, Lynn lives in Alabama with her handsome former-military husband, two crazy cats, and one spoiled American Saddlebred horse. Lynn's books have been called "exceptional and emotional," "intense," and "sizzling." Lynn's books have sold over three million copies worldwide.

To connect with Lynn online:
www.LynnRayeHarris.com
Lynn@LynnRayeHarris.com

Made in the USA
Middletown, DE
08 April 2018

when I couldn't get my own father to? There's a lot I'm only starting to understand about it, but I made a myth of him, and the myth wasn't real. I know that now because you are the realest thing I've ever felt, touched, known, and I'm not settling for less anymore.

Maybe I'm too late, and maybe that's what I deserve, but I couldn't live with myself if I didn't come straight to you (seriously, thank fuck for GroupMe and fancy friends) so I could tell you this. You are my *dream girl. The subscribers can find another one.*

I love you beyond belief,
Alex.

BITE THE HAND GOES META

(And This Time We Really Mean It)

A Satirical Short Story by Gus Moskowitz, Deputy Director

Here at *Bite the Hand,* I trust my in-house staff, contributors, photographers, and social media team to represent this brand the same way I trust my barista to know the ratios of a good cortado: intrinsically. I trust the people who built this platform to live out its mission every day. Even when it's uncomfortable. Even when it's awkward. And especially, especially when it's the right thing to do.

So, in the spirit of that trust, I'd like to tell you a story about a king who passed along his crown in exchange for the bigger, shinier kingdom next door. It's going to be uncomfortable, maybe a little awkward. You might make inferences.

Anyway. Here we go.

Gus's story is good, but then again, no one's ever accused him of not being a good writer. My favorite part is when the king's usurping little brother decides he'd rather be fed grapes on the coast than rule over anything. The story is chock-full of Easter eggs, witty clues, and subtle jabs. It is an exposé, and it is a work of fiction. It is damning, and it is innocent. It is pure genius.

I push open the front doors of the hotel, eyes searching the sidewalk for Alex as a brisk wind hits my tearstained face. After the past month, I'm going to have to double up on my retinol concentration.

"Alex?" My breath frosts into the air.

"Hey."

I turn and he's there against the wall, one hand in his pocket, the other holding his mom's articles, pink eared with wind in his hair. He looks calmer now. All the urgency is gone from his eyes. A man at rest.

I hold up the story first because talking about the letter right now will only make me start to cry again. "This will create a shit-storm."

Alex walks forward, shrugging. "It already has. I turned over my entire email exchange with Robert to Tracy Garcia before I came here. Plus, multiple board members called for a vote of no confidence in Dougie after Tracy broke the news to them."

I balk. "That was fast."

Alex nods. "A matter of hours," he says. "I wish you could have seen the fallout. Obviously, the deal with Strauss is off." He's right in front of me now, hot breath ghosting over my cheeks. The cloudy sky has started to spit noncommittal slush. But warmth still blooms in the center of my chest, sliding through my veins and into my fingers, all the way to the tips of my ears.

"What will happen to you?" I ask.

"I definitely need to be fired," Alex says softly, staring at my lips. "I'm shocked it hasn't happened yet, but then again, I *am* in a foreign country with no functioning cell phone."

I laugh, then abruptly stop when I realize: "The SEC is going to find you culpable of something," I say. "Hopefully just compensatory damages."

"Sounds like a good use for the trust fund."

"What about BTH? All your hard work?"

"The work's already been done," Alex says. "That launch will happen under a new CEO. I'm certain of it."

Slushy rain is turning his cheeks wet, but Alex looks unbothered.

"What now?" I ask.

My words break a spell, and Alex hauls me into a hug. His hand rubs soothing circles over the small of my back, coaxing me closer. "You tell me." He sighs, and the sound unfurls along my neck and ears. "I'm far from perfect. I probably need therapy, and I think I still want to freelance wherever the jobs are. Hopefully here. All that said, you tell me, Casey."

I breathe in his musky scent—like linens left in cold rain. It's different from what it was when we first met, but better now.

His lips graze the shell of my ear, and I say everything I mean: "Be with me."

We kiss like two starved and half-crazed wild things, so desperate to drink each other in that we both forget to breathe.

"Gonna take some time off," he mutters, fingers in my hair. "Lawyers, probably, and depositions, plus apartment hunting, for you, and—hiking."

"Hiking?" I gasp when his teeth graze my ear.

"Southern coast of England. I'm into hiking now, thanks to you."

I try to smirk against his chest, but my body is pulled taut, my emotions as stretched out as a limp rubber band. "Hiking would be good," I say lamely, trying to steady my breath.

He lifts my chin and says hoarsely, "Maybe our life together won't ever be steady or sure-footed. But I will *always* come back to you. You are my North Star, my safe harbor, and I love you so much I could die."

I stretch onto my toes and wrap my arms around Alex's neck. "I'm proud of you," I whisper to him. "I think you're brave. I love you, too, and I'll always be your home."

"I'm sorry you had to think I let you leave without saying good-bye."

I shudder. "You're here now."

"I'm here now," he agrees.

His trembling fingers trace my lips in reverence, and his mouth parts open when he leans in to kiss me. The last vestiges of winter chill expel from my body the moment our lips touch once again. He pushes his mouth gently against mine, tipping my head back and pressing his arm into the small of my back. It's the most romantic moment we've ever had. The rainy slush gets a bit more serious, but I can't feel it at all. There's only him, the perfect words shoved in each of our pockets, and a sense of calm that tells me we're exactly where we're supposed to be.

EPILOGUE

**Behind the Zines:
A Day in the Life of Casey and Alex**

Did y'all see they're dating irl???? There's a reddit thread!

Alex WOULD be the type to want flavor added to his (iced)
coffee (in the dead of winter)

The set of pink reusable utensils at Casey's greenhouse (i.e.,
cubicle), and how happy she got when she showed them
to the camera

I'm a sophomore in college and because of Casey I just
changed my major from Economics to Finance. Love you
Casey!

Did anybody see the SEC case against Alex's dad??? Fckn
wild!!!!!

Jack and Jill's wedding reception is all soft pinks and royal reds, with tall flower bouquets and four open bars. A chandelier made of carnations is hanging over the dance floor, and a disco ball at the arrangement's center spills light all over the refurbished Georgia barn while scorched cherrywood smoke drifts inside from the bonfire.

"This is different than I was expecting," Alex admits as I cut into my beef tenderloin, served to me *in my seat* (fancy) by a waiter with a sparkly bow tie (fancier).

"What were you expecting?" I ask.

Alex pauses. "That question feels like entrapment, and I'm not going to answer it."

I smirk. "Well, at least we're in a barn. And at least there is a dude in a kilt."

We both look over at the man in full Scottish formal wear: tartan, sporran, black knee socks, and all. One of Jill's distant cousins, apparently.

"But where are his bagpipes?" Alex grumbles.

"I beg you not to inquire."

"God, I was *starving*," Miriam groans around a mouthful of food.

"Same," Brijesh says. "A happy hour appetizer would have been nice. Maybe some croquembouche. Or tuna tacos. With microgreens."

"The nuptials started at seven thirty!" Miguel says. "Happy hour was already over. What we *should* have done was pregamed the ceremony."

"That," Sasha says, "would have been an abominably bad idea."

I turn to Alex, who's gone back to glaring at Lance—by far his favorite activity of the evening. We had an awkward introduction earlier (this time, Lance and his girlfriend didn't bail), but it's out of the way now, just like when I met Sonja.

Honestly, I only remember Lance is here every time I catch Alex staring at him like he could erase my ex-boyfriend if he glared hard enough.

"Alex?"

"Hmm?" He turns to look at me, arm coming to rest on the back of my chair.

"There's no need to feel jealous."

He doesn't look the least bit sorry or embarrassed by my chastising. His eyes darken as he looks at me—my eyes, my lips, my body. I feel his hand weave into my hair. "I don't feel jealous." His tone is at odds with his expression. "I feel protective."

"Oh, thank you for clarifying. By all means, glare on."

Alex bites the inside of his cheek, leaning toward me. "Let me have this," he says before pressing a kiss to my temple. "It's a new experience for me."

I shudder under his touch, annoyingly turned on. "Fine," I say. He laughs.

When we all get up to dance a few minutes later, Alex leaves his suit jacket on the back of his chair. We top up our drinks and head to the dance floor, getting silly and ridiculous and spilling expensive wine on our less expensive clothes. Eventually, Alex puts our empty glasses on the nearest table and spins me in the makings of a swing dance.

"They teach you this at Harvard?" I shout in his ear.

"Twelve-hour credit!" he shouts back.

"Could you have possibly fathomed that when we fake-kissed in Sleight of Hand, you'd wind up here as my real date?"

"Fathomed it? I made sure of it. Now I can say I've seen Atlanta beyond the airport."

The dance turns slow, and our bodies press in. I rest my head on his shoulder and let him hold me. "Are you having fun?" he asks.

"Of course," I say. "But I'll still be ready to go home."

I don't clarify which home I mean. Right now, it's London. But really, it's him. I trace the rose of Sharon tattoo on his forearm, and when I look back up, his eyes are twinkling.

Tracy Garcia fills the open CEO role at Little Cooper. Don is promoted to CFO, and Mrs. Cooper steps into the chairperson's seat.

For one reason or another, Robert Harrison is never named to the board of Strauss Holdings. He's never named anywhere, in fact, thanks to an SEC investigation suggesting he violated (*a*) his noncompete, (*b*) his confidentiality agreement, and (*c*) his fiduciary duty. But he gets no jail time. Go figure.

Alex puts in his resignation / is simultaneously fired, sells the Pottery Barn couch to Freddy, gives Cleopatra and Calliope to the guy across the hall, and kind of moves to London. (His mailing address is still his aunt's apartment in Queens, which I don't press at first because I'm not sure about the legal aspect of Alex living in a country where he's unemployed and not a citizen.) After three months, he picks up his first freelance job here, and that's when I ask him to officially move in by hiding his suitcase in the back of the closet and unpacking his things.

Gran *loves* him. She likes me fine (definitely more when I talk about finance, less when I talk about Dad or Tennessee or basically anything other than finance), and we get a meal together once every couple of weeks at very stuffy restaurants where I am required to wear something nicer than I wear to work. Once, she even invited a few other distant relatives, who are seriously awesome and therefore also on her shit list. But that woman fully thinks Alex Harrison is the best thing to happen to her since her daughter deserted their family thirty years ago. If Alex can't come, Gran is not interested. If we ever move again, I'll have to pry him from her cold, dead hands.

Like most other things, I grow into my job with time, and I think the job grows into me, too. I get to write a travel budget in the May issue. Alex prints it out and frames my first byline (which contains fewer than one hundred words but does include many numerical figures), then surprise-books the exact trip I budgeted—to *Morocco*—so we can take it in October.

There is one day at a pub near Bethnal Green where I have an allergic reaction and have to stick myself in the ass with my Epi Pen, right there at the lunch table. Alex is scarred so badly from it he stares into space for the rest of the day, even though I fully recover after twenty minutes.

We learn to cook together—because our apartment's stove actually works, and because we're trying to save for vacations. The result is a lot of burned things (burnt, if you're British) and bursts of laughter, and occasionally even a take-out order. But we forge ahead meal by meal, since every trip we take leaves us hungry for more. High on the list is a visit to Korea so Alex can show me another part of himself, but in the meantime, I've gotten to see the White Cliffs of Dover. I got a headache trying to keep up with an outdoor play of *Macbeth* on Oxford's spring grounds. Last month, we took a weekend-long flower-arranging class in Bath.

And no matter where we are, or how many times I go to the bathroom in the middle of the night, Alex always pulls me back against him so we can fall asleep in each other's arms.

ACKNOWLEDGMENTS

I feel profoundly overwhelmed to be writing acknowledgments for my first published novel. Mostly, because this might be the first time I've allowed myself to pause and consider *just how many* people believed in this book, and in me.

The first round of thanks goes to Melissa Edwards, my tireless agent, who pulled a manuscript with a voice and a concept out of her slush pile and gave that manuscript a desperately needed plotline. I frequently think back to that early draft and marvel at your ability to see potential and nurture it until it shines. Your guidance, advocacy, and understanding, before and after we sold this book, have blown me away. I can't wait to see what we achieve next!

Sallie Lotz, my inspirational editor—can I tell you a secret? When Melissa sent me the submission list for *Love Interest,* your name was right at the top. You pulled a manuscript with a voice, concept, and plotline out of your slush pile and gave it the lion's share of what makes a book compelling: emotion. I knew from the first time we spoke that you were the perfect editor to head into the trenches with. It isn't lost on me how diligently you worked on this book to make it the very best version of itself that it can be. I can't thank you enough for believing in the characters, and in me.

I have so much gratitude for the sensitivity readers who provided thoughtful feedback and invaluable insight!

To the entire team at St. Martin's Publishing Group, those I know by name and those whom I've never met but who still had a hand in bringing this novel to life: thank you from the bottom of my heart. Special thanks to Marissa, Austin, Brant, and Meghan, as well as to the production team, my fabulous copy editor, and any other sneaky helpers out there who are working hard behind the scenes.

Hannah Bonam-Young, my first author friend, the first person to scream in my DMs when she read my book: your friendship means a heck of a lot to me, and I'm proud of us both.

Thank you to every author that has shown me kindness on social media. I have felt so touched by you all for rooting me on, congratulating me, encouraging me, and showing excitement over my work.

Special thanks to my agent siblings, who welcomed me into professional writerdom with open arms, and to the Writing with the Soul community; the next time we get together in person I will *try* not to cry while spouting complicated metaphors about how much the community means to me, but no promises.

Endless love to my family:

Mom, who read my first novel (a thief-spy mystery adventure) when I was sixteen.

Dad, who told me I should read more books since I didn't know what "insouciant" meant (I overcorrected).

My sisters, Maddie and Amy, with whom I am the weirdest version of myself.

Grandma, who kept journals in my hand when I stopped writing, books in my hand when I stopped reading.

To my Charlotte friends, including but not limited to Mary

Caten, Sally, Maddy, Jenny, and Caroline: I adore you all. To my college friends, Lanna, Caroline, Katie, and Jordan: you guys are my literal heartbeat.

To Liza and Erin, two more of my best friends, who both inspired Miriam's character and are also the entire reason I can pretend to know anything about what it's like to live in New York City as a twenty-four-year-old with bigger dreams for tomorrow than five years from now. I hope I did you proud.

Lastly, to Morgan, my very own love interest. Romance readers joke all the time that nothing in real life can ever live up to a book boyfriend. But you prove that theory wrong all the time. Thank you for taking my writing career more seriously than even *I* did, in the beginning. I love you quite a bit.

ABOUT THE AUTHOR

Kelsey Shea Photography

CLARE GILMORE lives in Nashville, Tennessee. She spends her moonlight hours cooking excessively elaborate meals and planning more vacations than she'll ever be able to take.